KATELYN COSTELLO

The Frituals

First published by Katelyn Costello in 2018

First edition

ISBN: 978-1981463091

Cover art by Jane Farrell
Proofreading by Melanie Kirk

This book was professionally typeset on Reedsy.
Find out more at reedsy.com

For Grandma Costello, who taught me home was where you could get lost in many, many stacks of books.

Contents

Acknowledgement

To Ethan, for love, support and tough love talks.
To Babe Squad for being my cheerleaders from afar.
To my betas: Ethan, Chris, Alissa, Susanne, Lauren, and Alexis for helping the story become what it had the potential to be.
A special thanks to Mrs. Vogler for coming in at the end to make sure all was spic and span
To Melanie for making sure every word was just so.
Jane, thank you for all your help making this book look gorgeous, and spread its love.

1

Shauna

When she comes in, I am standing in a sea of skirts and bodices. Some of the fabrics are thick linens, tightly woven fabrics in soft shades of greens, blues and browns that hold their shape when thrown over a chair back. Other dresses are made of slippery silk that draw the eye with their vibrant hues. "Taytra, what do I wear?" I ask as I wade through the sea of fabric, looking for a dress to wear to the Fritual testing.

"I told you at lunch, it doesn't matter what you wear. After the water test, they have a change of clothes for you," my older sister replies from the doorway to our bedroom. She is in her signature red gown.

"Why am I given a new dress again?" I ask, discarding a soft yellow piece.

"What? All your research hasn't given you all the answers you need?" Taytra teases.

"Come on Tay. You know I've done as much as I can."

"Alright," she says, "I can tell you this." Taytra waits until I turn from the mirror. "You will need a new dress because you will have to get into the water. I don't know why they don't warn people beforehand, so they don't wear something that will be ruined. But I guess they want it to be more natural. They said something about letting the water react to you. I don't know why, it didn't really make all that much sense to me. I just know I went swimming, took a bath, and then went to an amazing feast where they told us we had all failed the test and none of us were the water Fritual. I think they wanted all the candidates to look the same."

"You got to go to a feast with mother and I had to sit here and do extra chores?" I ask, finally settling on a soft green dress.

"That may be what happened," Taytra says. "Hurry up, Father is waiting. You may have to go alphabetically, but we have to catch the first boat we can."

"I'll be quick," I say, turning from my sister and flinging the green dress over my underclothes.

I am struggling with the ties for the corset of the dress when Taytra calls from the hall, "Shauna let's go! We're going to be late!" She pokes her head back in and notices that I am struggling. "Father is waiting outside," she says coming up behind me to fix the dress. She heads back towards the door. "Come on we don't want to be late." I push a curl out of my face and hurry after her.

I step outside to see Father leaning against the fence that lines our property. He steps to the side to walk next to Taytra as we approach. Father strikes up a conversation with her, smiling and looking around at the sunshine; but behind those dancing eyes I can see that he was hurting. I know he wishes Mother was here to see me take the test. I wish she were here too. It has been a hard couple of months without Mother. The vision of her lying under the quilt she had spent months making, shivering, unable to keep down any of the food we tried to give her, was

2

burned into my mind. She came down with the flu and couldn't shake it. At least that was what the doctors said. We tried so hard to make her better, but no matter what we did she just seemed to get worse.

"Shauna," Taytra calls to me in her shrill voice, breaking me from the memory. "You don't need to walk so fast."

I pause and give them a chance to catch up. "Sorry, I'm just eager to get there. I didn't realize you had fallen behind."

"You were in your little world again," she says rolling her eyes. She turns to Father, catching her skirt in her hand, to stop from it getting tangled in her legs as she takes long strides. I'm guessing by the way she grips it she would have rather have worn pants or at least a shorter skirt, but when it comes to events like this Father has to be strict about what we wear.

"Father, do you think you could tell me the story again?" I ask watching birds dance on the path in front of us.

"I think I can do that," he says, with his soft, lilting voice bouncing off the leaves, wrapping them up in the story too. "Many years following the fall of Queen Chima and after Queen Moraine took her sister's place, Moraine drafted a treaty that ended the war. The rebel groups that had helped her stop her sister from destroying both races tried to return to their homes."

"A young elf named Matron and a girl named Serena struck up an unlikely friendship. Serena met Matron as a client through his blacksmithing business. As she was half elf- half human, she spent most of her life in fear that people would find her out. But when Matron didn't care, they became fast friends. Some, like Matron's Father, thought they were too close. Even in this time of peace, the races were still not content with each other. The two were advised to cut ties, but they continued to fight for their friendship; inevitably falling in love." Here, Father makes a face, scrunching it up playfully in fake disgust. He always gets so flustered when a suitor comes to the door for Taytra. He isn't ready to see us grow up and leave him yet. So whenever he gets to this point in the story, Father tries to pretend that love isn't all that it was made out to be. But Taytra and I know better, we saw him with Mother.

"Now Matron was gifted with the ability to control four of the five elements: earth, air, water, and fire. Only the descendants of royalty could control the last element, spirit. These descendants didn't have to take the throne, just be related to those on it. While most elves here were only able to control water, the Goddess blessed Matron with his extended abilities. The people didn't know how he was able to control so many magicks, So they created a name for this anomaly, a Fritual. With so many people hating their love, the young elf wanted to make sure his partner was protected. But he needn't have worried, Serena had her own set of skills. Her father was well trained in the art of sword play, who had taught her all he knew. Between the two of them, Matron and Serena made a formidable team."

"Serena and Matron were married, but in secret for their safety. Sadly, when their enemies did find out, disaster struck. Matron's father led an attack against his own blood. Matron was able to fight them off long enough to give Serena the time she needed to escape, but it cost him his life. It is rumored by some that Serena had a son named Amicus. A child that would continue the line, but no one knows who he was, or if he inherited any of his father's magick.

"It was discovered over time as our races mixed that humans block the magick making the offspring of an elf and a human

4

unable to control it. So the powers that were held in the time of old faltered. Legend says that Matron's blood and his magick run through the two races. After two hundred years, men and elves decided to test young people as they came of age for the presence of magick. We live at Cabineral Lake where seventeen-year-olds are tested to see if they have power over water." Coming to the story's end, Father smiles and turns to me. "Today you shall join the tested children."

"So what happens now that I have taken the test? What do I get to do?" Taytra asks eagerly, cutting off my attempts to ask questions. I let her roll over me. Someone is bound to be able to answer any of my questions today.

"I wouldn't sound so excited over there. There isn't anything special planned for those who have failed the test already. We just get to meet the candidates later and eat good food," Father says.

"So, what you're telling me is I have all day to do as much exploring as I want?" Taytra asks, a mischievous grin splitting her face.

I am pretty sure I know what she is going to be up to, but I'm not going to be the one to say it. But Father purses his lips and narrows his eyes, giving away he had already guessed it. "And just who do you think you will be doing this exploring with?" he asks, cocking an eyebrow at his eldest daughter.

"I was going to go looking for fabrics with Jacinta. She got an order for a new yule ball gown, and she needs to get some new fabric swatches," Taytra says spinning a web of lies as smoothly as she would run a brush through her wavy golden hair.

"Uh huh, sure. Would you lie to me if you had plans to go see that soldier boy?"

"Father, his name is Andrew. He asked me for one dance at Beltane. One dance! You just don't like him because he is a soldier. Andrew and I are just friends. Nothing more." She crosses her arms "he wasn't even a good dancer." She says quietly.

"All it takes is one dance. That's what it took for your mother and me." He misses a step as his thoughts turn inward for a moment. He shakes his head clearing away the past "I'm sorry. This day is meant to be about Shauna."

"Hang on, why are you so against him?" she accuses, quickly adding, "I don't want to be with him, but if I did why would you be so opposed to his presence?"

"Because he is training to be a soldier. We aren't in a time of war, we don't need soldiers. I don't see the point in training for something that isn't likely to happen anytime soon."

Taytra scoffs. "So what? There may not be a war coming but since he is training he gets to go and live in Cabineral City. He doesn't have to stay in this sad little town. He can go and make a better life for himself over there. I am proud of him. I hope he does well. Him and Ward, you don't seem to mind as much when it isn't your best friend's son."

"The city isn't as great as you think. It's a lot more expensive," our father counters.

She rolls her eyes. "Whatever, money isn't the only thing that is important to us."

"Us?" Father snaps, and I pick up the pace again. I don't want to listen to them bicker the entire way to the waterfront.

"Yes. Us. You, me, Shauna. Men. The race of man. Us. There are more important things to us than money," she says exasperatedly.

"Shauna, where are you going?" Father calls ending the fight.

"I was trying to avoid being seen with you," I say, waiting for them to catch up.

"I am sorry. That wasn't right of me, I should have paid more attention to you. It's—"

"It's my special day. I know." I say cutting him off. "Sorry, where do I have to go? I want to be there before they get to the D's, so I know I have plenty of time to get in the lineup."

"Your mother would have been so proud of you. I know you are hurting. You never show me an attitude." He pushes a lock of hair from my face and kisses my cheek. "You need to go to the first pier. They are splitting the alphabet into three to try to get the process to run a bit smoother. That means there will be three of you in the water at once. We," he points to Taytra and himself, "will be at pier six. They wanted to put the parents in the water far enough away that we can't shout things at you. Not that that makes any sense since none of us know what is happening when you get in the water. But we will see you at the banquet," Father says pointing to the crowd of people I am going to have to sift through. "We will let you get to it," he says, turning from me and glancing at my sister. "Tell me more about these fabric swatches."

She shoots me a look over her shoulder that could only be described as a desperate plea to help her escape. But I have to try to fight and find which pier 'Shauna Flynn' is going to be called from. I don't want to be late for the Fritual testing.

7

2

Shauna

The road from my home is closer to the fifth dock than the first. Which means that I have a bit more work to get to my assigned place than Taytra and Father. I am glad I had decided not to wear one of my dresses with a fuller skirt. There are nearly three hundred humans and elves all packed in along the boardwalk. Just as the children of man are tested every year, so are the children of the elves. I weave my way through all these people that talk in excited clumps.

The war of men and elves is long over, but many humans have never meet an elf before their testing. I have met elves several times before, last year being my most recent encounter, one of the many callers that Taytra had. The elf had been quite beautiful but as Taytra said, "I don't want to have the person I love, watch me die because they will outlive me for another two hundred years," which I thought was fair.

The elves around me are at least one hundred years old; I guess that is when they are deemed mature enough to be adults. To me, they look like humans a few years older than me, who have the natural glow of life to them. Like they always get a full night's sleep. Or like they never had to lift a pinky. Well they had those pointed ears too. I wonder if it is annoying to do their hair. Would it catch on their ears? I had once seen two elves lift a cart to help a man whose wagon had broken. They each took a side of the cart and lifted it, so he could slip a new wheel on the axle. They made what would have been hard for half a dozen men look easy.

From the looks of things, the piers are divided into three groups. The third pier was blocked by only elves, while the next two appeared to be for humans. That came as no surprise as the population of man has a much higher birth rate. Where the elves have twenty or so representatives the rest in attendance are the children of man.

I made my way through and found an elf in the pale blue of the queen's colors. "Name?" he asks, not looking up from the long piece of parchment in his hand.

"Shauna Flynn," I reply, scanning the crowds for anyone to talk to while I wait.

"Right," the elf shuffles the parchment up searching for the F's. "Ah, there you are, oh your birthday was just last month, happy birthday."

"Thanks," I say turning and seeing the person I am looking for.

"You are going to have a bit of a wait. About twenty minutes or so. We will call the letters E through H then assign you boats," he rattles off, already turning to the next person who arrived behind me.

"Thank you," I say walking towards a tree off to the side. I glance up and tilt my head towards the tree. We can talk without being jostled around here. I press my back to the tree, glancing over to my right to see the tall, dark boy, and catch his eye as he comes over. I turn quickly away from the soft brown eyes.

"What? Are we going to play coy now?" Philppe asks leaning against the tree.

"Well, there are a lot of people here. I don't really wanna bring attention to myself," I say looking at a group of elves as they take a boat out onto the water. They all sit with their backs so straight, I can't imagine that it is comfortable.

"Well maybe they should pay attention to you," he says. I can feel his gaze turn to me and feel my cheeks betray me as they go crimson. "What? Why does that embarrass you? Is it me or the idea of having to put yourself out there?"

I glance down at the hem of my skirt and kick away a small pine cone. "I still think it is crazy."

"Us courting?" I nod. "Shauna, I like you, I really, really do. You don't need to doubt that." He moves in front of me blocking my view of the crowds before us. Gently he takes my hand, when I try to pull away he says, "Let them look. Who cares? I know your father may not approve of me, but hey—" He nudges my chin up to look at him. "If I can make you blush like that because you feel you don't deserve me, I must be doing something right huh? Let me prove that to him."

"I guess I just—"

"Can we have letters C and D at pier two and E through H at pier one for sorting. Thank you," an elf calls using a sort of cone-like horn to amplify his voice.

"So much for twenty minutes." Philippe sighs and glares at the elf for a second for cutting off our conversation. "Please, meet me on the other side of the lake. I have something I want to talk about." I nod my consent, he bends and kisses my hand and gives it a squeeze saying, "I'll see you soon." Then he is off.

I don't really have time to wonder what he could possibly

have up his sleeve when I am carried by the sea of people over to the docks. The boat that we are meant to take is an old, worn out canoe. Its sides are a dark brown, waterlogged from years of sailing from one side of the lake to the other with those being tested to find the Fritual. The elf who paddles this particular canoe moves it as close as he can to the pier, so the edge bumps against it with the pull of the waves. He is kind enough to put a steady hand out to help my fellow passengers and me into the boat.

"What do we do for this test?" A young man whose last name is Hilton asks, peering over at the murky water.

The elf shrugs. It is a movement that seems strange for an elf to make but also looks entirely normal for this elf.

"How do you do a test if you don't know what to do?" the other girl in the boat asks. The elf shrugs.

"You are up first Miss Edward, as your name comes first," the elf says pointing to the girl.

"But what do I do?" He shrugs a third time. "Ugh" she grumbles and dives in with a large splash.

While I wait for the girl to resurface, I sit looking over the edge of the boat at my reflection. I watch her go down a few feet, swim in a circle, then head back toward the surface.

"Well, are you going to help me up?" she pants splashing around in the water as she struggles to get back into the boat.

I help the elf drag her up into the boat then glance over at the elf, who gives me a nod and I turn towards the water. I take a deep breath, filling my lungs with the murky, lake air before jumping in head first. Unlike Miss Edward, I enjoy swimming. I streak downward like an arrow, my hands forming the point high over my head, the weight of my dress helping to pull me down. At about ten feet under my downward pull slows and

I begin drawing the water with steady strokes. I have always loved the water, I spent many summers swimming and trying to scrub the smell of the lake water from my hair. As I reach the deeper water it becomes dark and murky, I glanced up at the surface, and I can see broken white reflections of the water. Fish slowly pass me as I begin to swim towards the right. Through the water, a dark cave comes into view. I quickly swim over toward it even though I'm starting to feel the tight pinch in my chest telling me I need air.

I'm feeling slightly lightheaded when I decide to take a look inside. I kick hard as the fabric of my dress bunches up around my calves. A small stream of bubbles escaping my lips when I accidentally kick the side of the entrance. When I look inside the dark opening, I am shocked by what I see inside. A beautiful girl with long black hair that fans out around her in the ebbing flow of water sits on a rock. Leaning back casually like she is bored of sitting down here in the depths of the lake. She has skin as pale as porcelain and dark, almost black looking eyes. But most striking is what she has instead of legs. She has a tail; the scales shimmering a soft green in the dim light. When she sees my head poke up around the edge of the cave, she pushes herself forward with her tail, so she hovers just below me.

"I am the Ragna, can you understand me?" Her soft voice is beautiful and captivating like the sweet bells that the children play on celebration days. My heart longs to stay with her in the depths and just take in her beauty, but my brain is starting to send frantic signals to my limbs urging them upward. "Take a breath," the Ragna says calmly taking in my upward glances. I stare at her aghast for a moment till she repeats: "take a breath." I shake my head, kicking back toward the entrance. "Shauna, please. You are meant to find me. But I need you to breathe. You will be able to, finding me was your first step."

I process this slowly, at least it feels like an eternity, either this whole thing is a hallucination, and as soon as I take a breath, I can rush to the surface this weird trance broken, or she is real and being serious. *How does she know my name?* I take a shallow, tentative breath. I am surprised when as I do so I feel a tingling sensation on the side of my neck and a bubble of relief in my lungs. When my fingers find the skin on my neck, they are met by three raised slices of skin. Gills.

"Wha—what?" I splutter my voice sounding muffled and strange under the water.

"I told you that you would be alright. I felt a difference as soon as you entered the water," the mermaid says. I had gone swimming in the lake before. Just last week I had gone swimming with Philippe but not once have gills appeared.

"Why? Why did this happen now?" I ask slowly, still trying to process the way that my voice sounds under the water. It is like a child's weak attempts at the flute compared to her's.

"It happened today because your powers have been awakened. It would only happen when the water magicks are strongest. Shauna, for obvious reasons, you cannot stay down with me much longer or people will begin to worry. So I will be brief, you, my dear, are going to meet with the queen today. Yes, you heard me correctly. The Queen, Moraine, will send for you. She will know what to do from there, but you must trust her completely."

"Wait, so does this mean I passed the test?" I ask stupidly pointing to her, to my apparent gills, and to the lake at large.

The Ragna smiles. "Yes my child, you are the one we have been waiting for."

3

Shauna

I break the water's surface coughing and sputtering, for effect more than anything. I am about twenty feet from the boat. Miss Edward whips her head around when she hears me and yells at the elf to get me. "Are you okay?" she asks as she helps pull me into the boat. "How could you hold your breath that long?"

"I go swimming a lot," I say shrugging one of the fluffy white towels around my shoulders.

I glance around the edge of the lake, looking for the bright sun from earlier that now hides behind a cloud. I catch Philippe's eye. He is on the shore where I had been a short while ago waiting to board his boat so he can go next. *Oh, Philippe,* I think, *I don't know how I am going to explain any of this to you.* All I can picture is his face crinkled up in confusion. Best not to tell him for now, not till I understand it myself.

I hop off the boat and watch the others that were in the boat with me head up the path towards the gates to the city. Philippe and I never actually established where we would meet, so rather than lose him in the city I decide to stay on the shore where I can keep an eye on him. I walk along the water a little way and notice a small pool of water were three rocks meet and the water collects within. Small fish dart around in their enclosure, dancing away from my fingers as I swirl them slowly around. I climb up on one of the rocks and slip off my sopping wet slippers, lying them on the warm stone to dry. Slowly I dip my toes into the fresh water and flinch away, a laugh spilling from my lips when I feel little fish nibble at my toes. I slip my feet back into the water, watching the scales flash as they weave around my feet.

I start trying to digest the information I just received. I am the chosen one of Cabineral Lake. I am the one who will be able to control water. It seems too unreal. I touch my neck where the skin had parted to reveal gills. Nothing. The skin is smooth. *Did they disappear as soon as I surfaced or just before? If I am the chosen one, what can I do? What can't I do? Is it why I feel so calm near the water?* Questions buzz in my head like bees. They swirl and swirl without end. My thoughts turn now to the actual test, for years, we have been making seventeen-year-olds just jump into the lake in the hope that they would somehow reveal themselves. I can't help but feel like that plan was flawed. There had to be a better way to show the powers a person possessed. Then again mine hadn't appeared till now.

I watch as Philippe executes a graceful dive into the water, slightly splashing his companion on the boat. After a short time, he emerges and climbs back into the boat. He looks disappointed, but of course, he would. Everyone will be disappointed. He shakes the water from his hair sending ripples scattering away from his boat. It's then that he spots me, and he breaks out into a broad grin.

I rise nonchalantly, struggling for a moment to slip the damp slippers back onto my feet, and tilt my head indicating where to meet. I see him nod in affirmation and my heart skips a beat. I move through the trees careful to hold my dress away from the branches and thorns that snag and pull. I look to my left and can just see the shimmer of the lake, while on my right there is a fallen tree. The sun has come back out, but its rays are softer here, the leaves dappling the beams. I hop up onto the tree, testing my weight before sitting and combing through my hair with my fingers. Once I have detangled it as much as I can with my fingers, I twist the strands into a braid and toss it over my shoulder.

When Philippe comes striding up the trail, I am lying down on the tree looking up through the leaves at the bright blue sky. His hair still shimmers with the droplets that won't let go. "Hello, Shauna." he says in his low, rough voice.

"Hello," I reply. He steps closer, our fingers interlocking before he raises a hand to brush away a tendril of hair away from my face. I'm shorter than him, only coming up to his chest, so I have to look up at him; it's something he says he likes about me. To look at him, he has to see my whole face. But here on my perch, I am almost eye to eye with him. The curl comes loose again, and he tucks it behind my ear, but, this time, he brushes his hand along my jaw as he does so, cupping my chin. Slowly he bends his head and kisses me.

My hands slide up his arms, his shoulders, and rest on his neck, my fingers lacing in his hair at the base of his skull. I swing my legs carefully off the fallen tree and slide down his chest until I am standing. He lays a gentle, fleeting kiss on my lips, then my nose and finally he comes to rest on my forehead pausing there before I sink my head on his chest and he hugs me close.

I can hear the thubump, thubump, thubump of his heart

through the coarse linen of his shirt. "Shauna, I have missed you so much," he whispers, and I can feel the heat of his breath on my ear.

"You're the one who went away," I mumble back inhaling his comforting scent.

"You knew I had to go; I needed to trade those goods for Father," he says running a finger over my damp hair. "But I am back now." He pauses, his hand coming down to cup mine. "Look at me Shauna; there is something I need to say."

Quickly I glance up at him, searching his face for signs of a problem. Carefully he reaches into his pocket and pulls out a small pouch. He had tied it with a piece of neat black cord. From the pouch, he pulls out a delicate silver ring, inlaid with blue stones. I just stare at the beautiful ring, enraptured by its many shining facets. "Leaving did give me a chance to find this, so it brought some good. Shauna, will you take it, will you take me and be with me forever as my bride?"

I glance from him to the ring, and back again as my sluggish brain puts the pieces together. "Yes! Yes! Absolutely!" I squeal throwing my arms around his neck, hugging him tightly.

Before I can take another breath, he is kissing me again more fiercely this time, and when we break apart, my lips feel slightly numb.

I touch my lips, still feeling the phantom pressure of his. It is almost like the phantom feeling of the gills that had been on my neck.

"Why what's wrong?" he asks his voice instantly softening. I shake my head.

"Nothing, absolutely nothing. I was just thinking how much I love you," I lie.

4

Taytra

After making a not so graceful dismount from the boat, Taytra waits for Father to climb up on the shore beside her. She has been here on this side the lake a few times over the years with her lessons or with Jacinta when she needed an extra set of hands for an appointment. So, while the grandeur of the city made many drop their jaw in awe she gives it a cursory glance and focuses on holding up her dress. She flinches whenever the cold fabric clings to her ankles. Of course the boat her father had picked has a hole in it. *Why wouldn't it? We had to take the first boat so we could watch Shauna jump in the water.*

"Where are you meeting Jacinta?" Father asks bending to squeeze some of the water from his pants.

"I told her I would meet her in the market on the south side. But I need to get dried off before I go do that," she says. "I think I saw her come up the path when we were in line from docking so I am going to see if I can catch up with her."

"Okay, just stay safe? There will be a lot more people in the city today." Taytra starts to interrupt him. "I know, I know you already know this. But I still need to say it."

She nods. "Okay, I am going to try to find her before I lose her. I'll see you at the banquet later."

"Go, have fun," her father calls as she hurries up the path.

She sees a few wet teens gathered in front of an inn. They are probably waiting for their room assignments for the afternoon.

"Hey Ward," Taytra says pausing by the crowd to say hello to one of the candidates in Shauna's lesson group.

"Hello, Taytra. Oh you would know, 'cause you did this last year? It can't have changed that much. This assignment we have to wait for? They give us a room, food, and a change of clothes right?"

"Yeah, you get this blue outfit to wear and get a bath, and last year they had some stew for us to eat."

He nods. "And let me guess, it makes it easier for them to keep track of all of us?"

"Exactly, not really sure what perks you get after you have already been tested."

"Name?" an elven woman asks coming up behind Taytra and tapping on her shoulder.

"My name is Taytra Flynn. I was tested last year so, I don't think I will be on your list there."

"Ah yes, you are correct." The elf's accent adding a gentle lilt to the words. "Unfortunately we don't have anything for you. Family members of the candidates must find their own quarters for the day. Now if you will excuse me." She turns to Ward. "Name?"

"Ward Hendricks," he replies sending a glance at Taytra that says *sorry you just got ignored.*

She shrugs and turns to go into the city. Maybe going to see if Jacinta is actually here wouldn't be so bad. She had said she might come over to take advantage of some of the deals she

19

could get when there were more people in the city. Taytra turns off onto a side street flooded with sunlight, she pauses near a fruit stand enjoying the feeling of the sun on her back. It won't be long until the leaves change and it got to be cold again. The selection of fruits the woman has for sale is sparse, it is clear that she is running low on summer supplies and is just waiting for the autumn harvest season. Taytra reaches into a small pouch that hangs from her waist and selects a coin or two for one of the small under ripe apples.

"Thank you dear. That will be two copper stones," she says grabbing a cloth to rub any dirt off the small thing.

"Thank you, I now have a snack to hold me over to the banquet." She takes the apple and makes a show of taking a bite into the hard flesh. The woman beams as Taytra turns away.

It only takes Taytra a few more bites to finish the apple. While it hits the spot she is sure she will be starving when it comes to the banquet tonight. She has been to the South Side Market a few times with Jacinta. When they had come before they normally would bump into one or two people. But now with the celebration of Mabon kicking off with the testing of the candidates, the sloping street is packed elbow to elbow with men and elves. Some are busy bargaining with the sellers, others like her are just using it as a way to kill time for the afternoon. As she looks down the hill toward the store Jacinta works with the most, Taytra thinks she sees the flash of her friend's long raven hair.

As she fights through the crowds to get to her friend, Taytra thinks of what it was like for her the year before. The test was annoying. Taytra hated the water. Shauna could spend hours in the lake swimming and relaxing next to the crashing waves, and Taytra wanted to spend as little time with the water as she could. So for Taytra the idea of jumping into the middle of the lake for nothing to happen, and to spend a good bit of time after dripping wet was one of the last things she wanted to be a part of. Honestly, the food wasn't worth it either.

5

Shauna

Philippe and I part before entering the city. He brushes one last kiss across my forehead and then walks through the gates. His stride is long, his arms sweeping along his body, his gaze scanning all around him like he doesn't have a care in the world.

I wish I could look as nonchalant as him, but inside my heart is reeling. I can feel the cool metal of the ring nestled on my chest, slowly warming next to my heart. We soon found that we weren't going to be able to do the exploring that we had wanted to do. Upon entering the city Philippe was pulled aside by some of his friends he hadn't seen since he had gone on the trip for his father, and I found that there were elves patrolling the city, looking for wet teens to send to inns to get cleaned up for the night. Taytra had told me about this, of course, but I had thought I would have a bit more time to look around.

"Name?" an elf asks, his eyes never leaving his scroll, already scanning before I had given him an answer. "Shauna Flynn," I say.

"Please follow me Miss Flynn." He takes me to one of the many inns that had been commissioned to house us for the day.

Won't he feel special later I think. *He got to take the Fritual to her inn. Yippee.* But I still don't feel special.

The inn he takes me to is large, with a thatched roof that looks like it needs to be replaced soon. The sign that hangs in front of it calls it 'The Dancing Leaves'. I turn to ask the elf what time I have to be ready by, but find that he has already spun on his heel and is twenty feet down the road. *Okay then* I think, turning and moving into the common room of the inn.

An elf who I assume is the innkeeper comes forward a scroll in hand. "My name is Mr. Fenster. How can I help you miss?"

"I believe that there should be a room for me for the day?"

"Name?" the elf asks already running a finger down the scroll before I say my name.

"Shauna Flynn."

The innkeeper turns to another elf in the room and waves him over. "This is Chicar, he will show you to your room. Her room is the corner one on the third floor."

Chicar nods and puts a hand up directing me to the stairs. "Thank you," I say with a quick curtsey and hurry to follow Chicar up the stairs.

"This is your room. If you need anything please don't hesitate to come down and get either myself or Mr. Fenster," Chicar says before exiting with a quick bow.

I turn to the door when he leaves and make sure it is locked before quickly stripping the damp clothes from my body. Just pulling the fabric off makes me feel warmer, and the sight of the still steaming tub of water waiting for me has me feeling giddy.

I sink into the welcoming arms of the water and lay my head back on the rim letting the heat soak my skin and into my hair. I glance around the room from my relaxed point. There isn't much in here, not that the candidates really need anything for the day. Just this tub, a bed, and a wardrobe. On the rim of the tub there is a thin white cloth and a bar of soap. I scrape the soap over my body as the heat seeps from the tub. Before I get cold again I climb from the tub and find a few towels in the wardrobe. I wrap my hair in one and dry my body in another.

On the bed I find a lumpy brown package. Attached there is a note that reads:

> *Dear Miss Flynn,*
> *These clothes have been generously donated for you from the court of Queen Moraine for the water ceremony that will occur tonight in the palace. This is where the announcement of the Fritual will be made should he or she be found.*

I untie the package and out falls a blue dress just like the ones that the other girls wore downstairs in the common room. As I slip the dress over my head, tighten the corset and, I find that it fits me perfectly. Like I am the only one that could ever possibly wear this dress. I tug the dress into place, fidgeting with the way it lays across my hips. Then I squeeze the water from my hair and secure it at the nape of my neck with a twist. *There, all ready for tonight. Well physically,* I think. I sit on the bed and pick up the scrap of paper that came with the dress to read it again when there is a knock at the door. I hurry over thinking it could be Philippe, but it is the elf Chicar.

"Oh good, you are ready. Mr. Fenster said that there is a coach waiting for you at the front of the inn," he said.

"A coach? For me? I didn't send for a coach, I don't have the money for one," I say in confusion, but as I say it I think back to what the Ragna said.

"That is strange," Chicar says, a frown curving his face in confusion. "I am sure that Mr. Fenster said it was for you. Do you mind coming down with me to double check?"

I nod and close the door behind me with a soft click. When we step into the room Mr. Fenster hurries right over. "Oh good you were able to come right down." The elf seems slightly nervous and keeps glancing toward the door. "Have you done anything that could get you in trouble with the palace? I don't want any trouble for my inn. Not right around Mabon."

He presses a piece of parchment into my hand with a loopy handwriting.

> To the Owner of the Dancing Leaves,
> I ask that you please send Shauna Flynn to me immedi-
> ately. A black coach shall be waiting for her outside the
> inn, following the arrival of this note.
> Queen Moraine

I don't know how to respond without making this elf panic for the safety of his inn, while also keeping my secret safe for the afternoon. "I don't know sir; I don't think I've done anything illegal. I would know wouldn't I?" But I do know, and it isn't illegal. I wish I could tell the innkeeper why I was being called so he would stop wringing his hands nervously.

"She doesn't like to be kept waiting so I would hurry on if I were you," he says.

I hurry outside, my skirts swishing as I do so. My palms are slick with sweat, but I don't want to wipe them on the delicate fabric. Outside a sleek black coach waits for me. An elf in fine clothes opens the door. I give him a quick once over and when I hesitate he waves me on. "It is alright Miss, I know who you are. Lord Damian gave me explicit directions to protect you with my life." He smiles when he sees me hesitate and try to remember from my lessons who Lord Damian is. "The head guardsmen, my master," he supplies. "Can't be failing him now can we?" I nod and climb in. The coach-elf helps me in then closes the door behind me leaving me in unexpected darkness. It takes a moment for my eyes to adjust to the dim light.

"Miss Flynn," a voice says from the corner. I squint into the darkness barely able to make the silhouette out of the woman sitting in the corner.

"Um yes, I'm Miss Flynn."

"I am the advisor to the Queen. Pull the curtain back a crack you will see I speak the truth."

I bump into the carriage wall as we go around a bend, drawing the curtain back a bit farther than I meant to. Light pierces the inside of the carriage blinding me for a moment. The queen is easily distinguished by her flaming red hair; this woman has dark brown almost black hair "I'm sorry, who are you? You look familiar for some reason but I know I have never met you before. I mean why would I meet anyone from the palace before now?" I bumble the words spilling out in what I hope is a coherent thought.

"I am Serena Nightcastle, I am known as the Guardian," she says in a cheery tone, different from one as important as she is.

"Oh, I have seen a sketch of you in my books. That is why I know you." I say excitement pulling the words from my lips before I realize how silly that sounds.

"Yes, and I will answer all the questions you can think of in good time. I know that there are many that would want to ask me things, especially in your case," the half-elf says.

"Are you my..." I start trying to puzzle out my possible relation to this woman of history.

"We won't get into that today," Serena says quickly drawing me back from the edge. "Now, you are going to tell me if you saw anything in the lake when you took your test this afternoon."

"I— well um— I was told that— I mean I read that you aren't supposed to tell anyone but the queen what occurred during the test."

The elf-woman laughed. "Smart girl, but I assure you, that you can tell me what happened." I slide slightly as the carriage rolled to a sudden stop, with the sound of stuttering hooves from the horses. "I think that we are back. We can talk more inside. Come."

6

Jamie

After dropping Shauna off to the test, and Taytra goes to apparently find Jacinta, their father passes through the gates and heads to a pub he has frequented several times over the years. The streets are milling with people, but not in way that makes his travels difficult. Jamie watches a few elven children who look to be around nine or ten, but for all he knows these children could be the same age as him. They aren't tall enough to see over the crowd, so they dart between people trying to push their way through. He watches one girl scurry up a tree, she balances on the tree branch, pigtails swinging. Some kids sit on the side, these children were either too young to understand or, who had gotten bored watching the same thing happen over and over again over a hundred times.

"Sir," one child says coming up to him. "Sir, do you know how the testing is going? My brother is at the test this year, but Mother wouldn't let me go." He crosses his arms and kicks a stone along the ground. "She said my time would come and that I just have to be patient." He looks quite annoyed. "I just wanted to understand why everyone made such a big fuss about it."

"Well, do you know what they do for the test?" the man asks the little boy who shakes his head. "You are not alone. No one knows what the test is exactly, even the people doing it. All they tell you to do is jump in the water to dive down. That's it. So your brother probably jumped in then got back in the boat. Then you go to the city and take a bath and wait for the ceremony. Have you heard about the ceremony?"

The little boy seems to vibrate with excitement "Yes! Mother said it's a giant feast with hundreds of different foods. More than I could ever imagine! I can't wait to be old enough to go to it. Is the ceremony better than the test?"

Jamie laughs wondering just how long it would be before this small elf would be able to go. "If it is anything like how it was when I took the test, then yes. The ceremony is better than the test. You get to see the palace and see elves and the queen!" The boy's eyes get as big as saucers. "Then we get to see lots of food, it is all prepared by the queen's cooks, so it is very yummy. But shhh," Jamie says leaning down closer to the boy who creeps close on tiptoes. "You wouldn't want your mother thinking you were bugging people now would you?" The boy stands up straight as a pole; he glances around. When he sees his mother isn't anywhere to be seen he gives Jamie a mischievous smile, he makes a motion of zipping his lips and throwing away the key before scampering off down the road.

"Jamie! Jamie Flynn!" a man calls from down the street. He is a squat little man with a cane. He presses his weight into the ground, hobbling up to Jamie.

"Hello, Omar how are you?" Jamie asks shaking the man's hand.

"I have been well. My leg isn't giving me too much pain lately thanks to that doctor of yours. Thanks again for the recommendation. How are you? Where are your girls at?"

"We have been doing well. Tay is off to who knows where and Shauna is being tested today. It definitely has been a change since Marion died but we are doing well all the same." The two turn down the road, and Jamie sees the inn. "Would you like a drink?"

"I would, thank you," Omar says with a hearty laugh. "The Goddess knows I don't get out enough for a drink."

They go down the road as quickly as Omar can get across the uneven cobblestones. They find a table near the bar and Jamie grabs two pints. He slides the tankard across the table and takes a swig of the foamy drink. Jamie puts the tankard down with a small thud and wipes his mouth with the back of his hand.

Omar takes a hearty gulp of ale then says, "By the Goddess! That is crazy, both your little girls tested. They are almost women grown. I remember when they had their first lessons! Wild blond hair falling out of braids and matching dresses so you couldn't tell them apart."

Jamie smiles at the memory of his two little ones. "Marion and I used to call one and then the other trying to figure out which was causing trouble. We never seemed to call the right name out."

"Oh come on, you know that Taytra was the one who was always causing the trouble."

"I try to give them each the benefit of the doubt, but yes it was Tay most of the time," Jamie replies, his lips quirking up in a broad grin.

"Ward is taking the test today too. I forget that he and Shauna are in the same lessons."

"He seems to get on with Tay pretty well," Jamie says.

"Well they would, they both have big personalities and know

what they do and do not like. And don't seem to be afraid to tell you." Omar swirls the drink around a few times watching the bubbles, nearly spilling it. "I don't see him too much now. He does a lot of training. He wants to try to get into the queen's military. He heard that elves are willing to take some humans into their core. So he wants to do that."

"But?" Jamie asks sensing his friend isn't thrilled with this idea. "You know I am not keen on the idea, but Ward is your son, you don't need to feel like you can't express your pride when you're with me."

"I don't know," he says rubbing a hand across his forehead. "I want him to do what he wants to do, and I believe that he could be a great soldier but, I know I won't see him if he leaves. You know how things are with Pat, I need someone else to talk to besides her always checking to see if I am okay. I am fine. I just— I need another man in the house." He shakes his head. "I don't know. Any suitors lined up for the girls yet?" Omar says changing the subject.

Jamie shrugs. "A few have come by for Taytra. But there isn't any that stick around for long. Shauna is talking to that Philippe boy. The merchant's son. I am not thrilled, but she seems happy, so I guess I have to live with it for now. I'm glad, to be honest, that nothing seems too intense with either of them. I am not ready for them to leave me yet. They are my only family. I don't know what I am going to do when they leave. Maybe I will move into town. It would be easier than me walking from the farm every day for the Bakery."

Omar nods. "I think that would be a good idea; then we can get a pint more than every few months," Omar says before taking a sip. "I need to empty your pockets a bit more."

Jamie laughs. "No, sir you are not going to pass your tab onto me." He gets up. "Come on; I'll get you one more drink. Next round is on you sir."

7

Shauna

I have so many questions buzzing in my head as we pull into the courtyard of the castle. I have so many things I want and need to know, but I know I need to hold my tongue. We hear the driver climb off and come round to the door. The door opens filling the dark interior with bright sunlight. "Ladies," the man at the door says with a bow. "We have arrived at the palace." The Guardian nods her thanks as he helps her gracefully down. I, of course, follow behind. I feel like a lost puppy.

An Elven guard whispers something in Serena's ear as we make our way through one of the curving passages. I am in awe of the grand place. The ceiling reaches up at least a hundred feet in some rooms to large vaulted ceilings with majestic drawings of long ago times. In my distracted walking, I almost run into Serena when she stops. She has brought me to a small council room.

A long table made of a dark brown wood fills the room. Six high back chairs surround the table, each intricately carved with a symbol on the top. The most extensive chair at the end made of a lighter wood with large spirals, small flowers and other designs covering the high back.

A small elven woman steps out from behind the chair. My mind takes a few seconds processing how shockingly beautiful she is with her porcelain skin, bright blue eyes, and vibrant red hair, that I didn't realize who it is at first.

"Please sit," the Queen says as she settles herself and her skirts into the pale chair.

I sit feeling like a mouse in the large chair. "Well, um— Queen I – I mean your grace!" I stumble and feel a flush creep up the back of my neck.

"Don't fret yourself, my dear, if it helps you to feel more comfortable you may call me Moraine. I am sure in the future we will become close friends," she says laying a comforting hand on mine. "I am here to be your friend." She sends me a soft, comforting smile across the table. "Please explain to Serena and me what you went through with the test."

"I am now your equal?" I squeak, she just nods waiting for me to continue. Though I would really like to pause and focus a bit more on that point. "Alright, Mor—Moraine," I say slowly testing the name on my tongue. I glance toward Serena; she waves a hand gently coaxing me to continue. "Well, you were right. I did see something when I was in the lake." A smile plays at the corners of the queen's lips, but she says nothing. I plow on, "I was swimming around just looking. But at the same time, I didn't know what I was doing. Curiosity got a hold of me, and I had to see what was in this cave. There I found a mermaid called the Ragna; she showed me that I could breathe underwater. She also said that I was the chosen one and this was just the tip of what I would be able to do." I jump as an elf comes around the back of the queen's chair.

The queen glances behind her casually and says, "Now

Damian, what have I told you about sneaking up on me especially when I have a guest." She says, though there is clearly no scorn in her voice.

"I am sorry your majesty," he says but he doesn't sound sorry to me. "I came to tell you that it is time to get ready for the ceremony. All my men have been prepped, do you have any additional requests?" he asks glancing at me.

"Thank you, Damian. Shauna, this is Damian, he has been a member of the High Guard for years I recently promoted him to Master of the High Guard. He served my Father, may his soul rest in peace, then, when I had my coronation, he swore an oath to protect me. Especially after the chaos that my sister created with her short reign. Damian is my main protector, but also my adviser. I think," she says turning back to him, "you should advise them to begin high alert, and post more people at the exits."

"It will be done your majesty," he says with a ready bow.

"Shauna, you shall go with me. You can finish telling me what you know while I get ready in my rooms."

I follow the Queen to her chambers, Serena flanking me, and try not to look to out of place as Moraine's ladies in waiting take her to another room. She leaves the dark gray dress, and they help her into a fabulous deep blue one. The room is large, open, and airy. Its high ceilings come together at a point, from which a large crystal chandelier hangs. Serena and I wait until they finish buttoning every tiny silver button up Moraine's back and the ladies in waiting leave before continuing to tell her about the things I saw in the lake. "My lady, I don't know what I am doing. I have never had gills before. I have never been able to breathe underwater. What makes now so different?"

"We believe, at least what the elders who are still able to

practice say, is that it is a combination. As we elves celebrate
Mabon this week, we dedicate several ceremonies to water; the
lake test has just become one of those rituals. So in this time
of magick and tradition, it is believed to more clearly reveal a
Fritual. The second is influenced by you. Elves used to develop
powers at different rates; we test at the time when powers have
become the most obvious in the past. What will your powers be?
You may have been able to hold your breath for a long time in
the past, now you can breathe, or you were a strong swimmer,
now you can shape the water around you to push you through,"
the queen says sitting in a chair and arranging her skirts around
her in a gentle arc. "What is your next question?"

I glance at Serena. "Well? I guess why me? Why not my sister,
she is older after all. She took the test, why doesn't she have
any powers?"

"I believe I can answer that one," Serena says guessing my
other question. "Yes, Shauna there is a chance we are related.
But in the four hundred years since I had my baby, there hasn't
been much time for me to extend the line. If my son has, that
is his bidding. So there is a chance you are a direct descendent
of Matron. So there is a slim possibility that in time you could
learn a second magick. However, you could just be blessed by
the goddess. She may have looked into your heart and seen
goodness and chosen you. You have earned the title Fritual
today. You are chosen."

"I don't really feel blessed," I mumble.

"You may not feel worthy now," Serena says, "but in time
as you begin to understand your powers more, you will." She
smiles. "My Matron was the same way. He hid his powers for
so long but once he embraced them no one could stop him."

Except the Dark Ones that killed him, his own Father I think.

A knock at the door makes all three of us jump. "Enter," Moraine says.

A servant enters and bows. "You are needed downstairs. Those who have gone through the testing have all gathered below the gates."

"Alright, I will be there shortly. Please remind Damian that I want the guards on high alert."

"As you command, your grace." The servant bows and quickly makes his way from the room.

Serena turns to me. "I have something I want to discuss with you. Something I want you to know is not going to be easy but from experience may be the best thing for you."

I feel a pang of unease in my stomach. "Yes?"

"For a long time, before Matron was known as the first fritual, before I knew him, he hid the person he was to try to learn who he was. You don't really have that option, but it might be good for you to do after tonight," she says slowly gauging my reaction.

"You want? You want me to go into hiding?" I say, the words feeling like they were falling out of my mouth.

Moraine looks more serious then ever. "I have reports of darkness brewing. I am working hard on getting official reports but no one has come back yet." She pauses glancing at Serena. "We want to be able to keep you safe, give you a chance to train and understand what is happening to you. It will also help to ensure that your family is safe. At least we hope a separation will do that."

"But, my mother just died a few months ago, if I leave it will tear my family apart!" I say.

"I know it will be very hard," Serena says, "but I would hope your family will be understanding. It would only be for a few months. And you would just stay here in the palace, just like Matron did. You won't be shipped off somewhere."

"I don't care, how does that make it any better? So what they are across the lake. If you keep me here and won't let me go see them what is the point?" I feel my mouth turning to sand paper. "I can't do this. I won't!"

Moraine turns and slips earrings through her ears. "My dear, I know there isn't a lot of time for you to process this." Her voice is firm, almost patronizing.

I shake my head trying to stop the tears from forming on my eyelashes. "No," I say to her and to the tears that try to fall.

"But it is time you became known and take your title." With a gentle hand she reaches up and wipes away a tear. I pull away and she smiles a sort of half smile. "I know you will be astonishing."

My heart pounds in my chest. *I want to go home.*

8

Shauna

Serena brings me down a side passage so no one will know that I have been with Moraine. We hurry down the stairs using a few servants as cover. "I'll see you later," Serena says before disappearing back up the stairs.

I try to step lightly and to look as excited to be there as the other candidates as I merge in with the crowd. You would think acting as if I was in awe would be natural. But I know the smile on my face has to look fake. My stomach is a seething pit of nerves and anger. I can suddenly do a form of magick no human has ever been able to do, and, the people who will teach me how to use it correctly want me to renounce my family. Looking happy is the last thing on my mind right now. Though masking my feelings is something I probably will have to get used to.

I push through the crowd until I find Ward, one friend in a sea of faces, and we sit together for the feast shoulder to shoulder with the other candidates. I have never seen such a rich array of food: potatoes, glazed carrots, chicken, turkey, four different types of biscuits, and rolls. I try to eat, but my nerves have taken away my appetite.

"What's the matter with you? You usually eat more than I

do," Ward observes as he reaches across the table and grabs another buttery roll.

"Nothing is wrong, I'm just nervous," I say a little too quickly. Ward gives me a look that says he doesn't believe me one bit. "Really," I say with a bit more composure. "You know I don't like award ceremonies." He gives me another scornful look and is about to say something when a bell tolls, telling us it is time to move on into the main ceremony.

We rise as instructed by the elf at the head of each table and move to another room. The seating is alphabetical by our last name, while the adults get to sit pell-mell in the back. Ward, whose surname was Bacorn, is in the second row, I being a Flynn, am about halfway through the crowd, Philippe being a Mattick is a few rows behind, sitting on the aisle. When I sit down, I make sure to find Father, Taytra, and Philippe in the crowd.

We sit talking for a few minutes while the hall settles down. But I feel the fear of the next few minutes sitting in my stomach like a stone. I tap my foot, the little heel clicking incessantly on the floor. The girl to my left glances from the tapping of my heel to the way I am wringing my hands. I feel my face burn as she stares hard and shove my hands under my thighs still feeling the need to move.

"What is going on with you?" Annoyance and concern mingling in her voice.

A single trumpet blast sings through the air sparing me for the moment but proclaiming my doom. Then a door at the top of a short staircase at the far end of the room is swung open. Everyone turns shifting in their seats to try to get a glimpse of the famed Elven queen. They freeze, mouths agape at her beauty. Moraine moves forward, standing on the little landing at the top of the stairs smiling down on them all. Then all at once, everyone seems to remember that this is the queen and rises quickly to their feet. I hurry to follow them, every part of my being pulling me down, trying to force me to lay down and hide under the chairs, to crawl between them and out the doors.

Moraine walks to the front of the hall, long gown trailing behind her, the fabric spiraling around her as she turns back to face us. The long sleeves of the dress slip down her arms as she raises her delicate hands and signals for all to sit. She smiles and scans the crowd around her, locking eyes with me for a brief moment before moving on.

"Yet another year has passed, a year of peace and prosperity between our two races. Our young grow older and wiser and each day brings new life. Today our young around the lake were tested just as they have been for three hundred years. Each year the question arises, and it is time to give the answer we await every year. So I ask you now has the chosen one of Cabineral Lake been found out today?"

As she speaks, the energy level in the room grows higher and higher on every word, the people seated begin to murmur and turn to each other talking excitedly. I glance at Father, and I see that he knows like all the parents who have sat where we are sitting, that this time is different from all the others. But I am the only one in the crowd who knows why.

Moraine waits with hands clasped elegantly in front of her until the crowd falls silent. Slowly the crowd turns back to face her. They remain in silence for what seems to be an eternity, and I know this is it. My life is about to change. There is no going back now.

"I have ruled as queen for a little over five hundred years.

My life is old and filled with the war of our races. But by our race, I am considered young. I have much to learn. The old tale you tell about Matron and Serena occurred as I was rising to power. When it became known that the merging of our races caused a death of Magick, I had a dream for some time that I would be the one that revealed the next Fritual of Cabineral. The next individual blessed with powers like we haven't seen in generations. But part of me knew that I might not be the one." A murmuring broke out again, and she raised a hand, and silence resumed. "First I would ask my dear friend to come forward and reveal herself."

Serena steps out of the shadows to the queen's right, always guarding her even in secret. Cries of surprise and awe break out throughout the crowd from both men and elves. Moraine continues, her voice amplified by magick. "This is my dear, devoted friend Serena Nightcastle. Some of you might know her as The Guardian. She has stood at my side for nearly three hundred years. She was the wife of the most powerful elf we have ever known, Matron, who controlled four of the five elements. Serena, do you sense a renewal of your husband's power?"

Serena nods, "I do, and I have met and spoken with the candidate. They are young but wise. Scared but courageous. Quick to act, but thoughtful. I believe they will use their powers for good."

Moraine nods in agreement turning to the crowd. "Would the Fritual of Cabineral Lake, and my newest friend please come forward? Come and claim your destiny!" she shouted, voice echoing in the arches of the hall.

A measure of stunned silence hangs over the air, and I panic, fearing that they will revolt or do some other terrible thing when a roar of delight and excitement fills the hall with a cacophony of noise. I can't move, I am pinned to my chair by fear.

Someone shouts, "Well, where are they!?"

I glance up and see Moraine and Serena looking at me, hands outstretched, beckoning me forward.

I feel cold, like ice as I rise, my hands shaking, I don't want the world to see that, so I make fists digging my nails into my hands, already feeling the half-moon indents.

"What are you doing?" the girl says trying to grab my hand as I try to push my way past her. "Wait— oh my gosh! It's you!"

I nod and step away from her. The rest of those around us realize like she did, what is happening and begin a cheer pushing me along the row till I stumble into the aisle. "Shauna! SHAU- NA! SHAU-NA!" they cry, the sound carrying me to the queen. She takes my hand and squeezes it. Kindly she doesn't acknowledge how clammy my hand is.

Then she raises her hand and again all in the hall fall silent. "This is Shauna Flynn. The Fritual of Cabineral Lake. She has a rich history of benders behind her to follow and a wide road before her." She turns to me "Shauna would you like to say something?"

"I was chosen—" my voice cracks, and I try again. When I look down and see all the eyes on me, I close my eyes. "I have been chosen to be the Fritual of Cabineral Lake." I take a deep breath gathering the courage to blatantly disobey a queen. "I don't know exactly what will happen in the next few years. But," I open my eyes and find Philippe in the sea of faces who stare at me in awe, I watch as some slowly turn to horror, pity, and sympathy. "But I know I will be so much stronger, with those that love me by my side supporting me."

43

I hear Taytra and Father saying something and turn to address them when Moraine cuts me off. "What Shauna means is, she knows she will be so much stronger knowing those that love her support her decisions to leave and protect herself and them."

"And— and for right now I need my family by my side as I go through this transition," my voice cracks and fades away.

The crowd shifts like the waters of the lake as they sense the tension between us. I can't look at Father, but I know he is rushing forward. He cries out to me, but tears are filling my eyes blurring everything into a sea of blue. I can't look at him, I can't see him anyway. "I can't do this. This isn't happening, this isn't happening." I take deep heaving gasps trying to calm myself as I feel all the eyes boring into me.

"Shauna what the hell?!" I hear Taytra shout. "Get off me, I need to get to my sister." I hear a thud as she punches a guard.

I sob, covering my face.

I want to turn away. "Shauna?" he asks softly, feet from me halfway up the staircase. "Shauna just listen to me. Focus on me, breathe. We will figure this out."

"I am afraid the decision has already been made," Moraine says kind but firm. Like she actually has my best interest at heart. "We have rumors that the Dark Ones are on the move. Some have even been spotted outside the city. Even they could feel that the magick was different this year." She glances behind her at Serena. "We don't want to have to have the guards remove you. Just let us finish the ceremony so we can move Shauna to a safer location. If there are Dark Ones here you are just prolonging her exposure."

"Please just stop for two minutes," he asks with the same firm tone. Those in the crowd murmur again as Philippe is recognized

Moraine is taken aback. She clearly is used to people following her every word. She hasn't had to deal with a person like Philippe in a long time.

"You don't have to do this. We can get out of here and live somewhere else. You don't need to accept this role," he says wrapping me in his arms.

"Philippe, don't you see? I have to; I can't just run away from this. This is too important."

Anger and pain flash across Philippe's eyes. There is a depth to them I have never seen before it scares me, but I can't quite tell why. "Shauna, I love you, but I don't think this is something you should do," he says.

"If I don't who will? I might be the only one able to be the Fritual."

"Why didn't you tell me earlier? You were with me after the test!" Philippe asks. He glances around. "Look can we finish this conversation somewhere else?" he asks Moraine. But by his tone it isn't really a question.

I take a deep breath gathering strength and willpower. "I have a gift, a gift that if I can use to protect our people I will. I want to do it."

People murmur, I hear their whispers, I hear the pain they feel for me. I hear their doubt.

"Philippe I am going to ask you once more to step back. We need to finish the ceremony," Moraine says.

Philippe openly glares but steps back keeping me within arm's reach.

Moraine hands me a silver goblet of water. She raises a hand to silence the murmurs, trying to continue the ceremony. But the crowd has already frozen mid-word staring at me, the doubt disappearing from their lips. The water rises from the cup in a spherical shape floating a few inches from the rim before collecting back into the cup.

My eyes are fixed on the cup trying to see if I imagined it. I feel tired like I've spent all day walking through the city. *What made the water float? Was that me?*

Distantly I hear, "Shauna that's amazing," and feel Philippe put a hand on my shoulder. It's warm. His hands are normally warm but this, this is hot. It burns, I am burning, flames are licking at my dress. I turn in shock as screams break out in the crowd and I start beating the flames away from my skin. I dump the cup of water on my shoulder leaving it a soaking mess of blue and black scorched fabric and angry red skin.

I turn to him as the guards grab him, but he doesn't fight. He, like everyone else in the hall, is staring at his hands. Philippe's hand glows an angry red like it is still burning. I cringe away from him as he reaches out to me trying to apologize. "Shauna I— swear I never knew— I could— I am so sorry." He splutters pushing his hands as far from me as he can. "What is happening?"

Moraine gracefully steps between the two of us. Voice no longer as kind. "Philippe! Fire and water do not mix."

I step away from Philippe and turning away from the crowd give myself a few seconds. I hear him trying to push past the guard that comes forward to protect my back. "Philippe!" I say sharply turning to face him, not bothering to wipe the tears away. I pause when I notice what is happening in front of me. As my tears fall from my cheeks, they gather together before me like there is a gravitational pulling them all together. I don't know what I am doing or how but, I am still able to manifest this orb of water.

I glance up at Moraine in surprise, when I see him. Damian stands behind the Queen, his dagger inches from her back. "No!" I shout and point at Damian, launching my orb at him. Physically all it does is shock him, but it is enough for him to drop the dagger with a cry of surprise, and I rush and snatch it up holding it out in front of me.

A murmur breaks out around the hall when those gathered realize they have just seen an assassination attempt.

"Damian?" Moraine asks taking a step back while holding the position between him and me. Serena takes a step in front of me, a hand reaching to grab a blade that lay against the small of her back. The guards moving to flank her.

His face splits into a cruel smile. "There may be Dark Ones here, let us move her so she isn't exposed," Damian mocks. The hall falls deathly quiet. "Every year we have waited patiently for the chosen one to come. It was simply a matter of time. We are in every kingdom. We are the ones blocking your communication to the others. I always thought your sister was right. The elves are the superior race. And these humans are just tainting our power. She is living proof!" He turns toward me another dagger appearing in his hand.

I take an involuntary step back and try to think of what to do. *How did I make the water do that before! I don't know, Goddess my shoulder hurts*, and I am tired, so tired. My arms shake from the weight of the knife though seconds before it was light. I take another step back, and my knees buckle. Moraine steps to my side, and Serena comes in front of the two of us.

"Stupid girl," Damian sneers, "if I don't kill you, you will die trying to cast spells well before you are ready."

"I am stronger than you think." Forcing myself to my feet. I hear Philippe struggling against the guards behind me. *Please just let him go. He just wants to protect me.*

"I am sure," he says scornfully.

Before I can make another comment Taytra is flying into motion, she is on the stage and grabbing the loosely gripped dagger from my hand. "That is my sister you are threatening! That is not going to happen!" she hisses before plunging the blade into Damian's chest.

"Who do you think you are?" he croaks, staring down at the blade.

"I am the Fritual's big sister. And I will always protect her." She shoots a look at Moraine before yanking the blade out of his chest and plunging it into his neck. "Always." She hisses.

"Tay!" I cry and pull her back as in his dying movements he lashes out, his hand transforming into a hand with inky black claws.

We hold each other and watch as he falls to his knees. He stares at me. "You will not escape us, Shauna Flynn."

Clutching feebly at his neck Damian falls to his side in a bloody heap. Inky black magick stains his blood. The other guards in the room hurry the crowd out of the hall and away from the Queen before more damage can occur. I sink to my knees as Taytra clutches me.

In the corner of my eye, I see him still standing there, forgotten after Taytra's attack. "Philippe, I am so sorry." I whisper as the room swirls away into blackness and I sink deeper into Taytra's arms.

9

The Sisters

When I wake up the fabric of the bed I lie on is stiff with starch and smells of medicinal herbs and spices used by the elves.

"I think she is waking up, Father!" a familiar voice says eagerly.

"Are you awake Shauna?" Father asks, but something is missing from his usual greeting.

"Mentally or physically?" I ask with a smile as I sit up against the pillows. Neither of them smiles.

After a very long pause, Father asks slowly, "Did you know there was a chance you could be the Fritual before last night?"

I shake my head hard feeling childlike as I did so.

"Okay, first Shauna; I cannot continue our conversation without first telling you that you will not see Philippe for a while."

I feel my face drain of color "why what happened? Is he okay?"

Father raises a hand halting any further questions. "The elves have taken him to Fueguasta peak for testing. I would have to agree with them that based on his show yesterday, he could be the Fritual that can control fire."

I nod, my head still feels like it is spinning. "Oh okay, uh can I have a glass of water or something to drink?"

"Sure." He leaves me for a moment and returns with a cup of water. "So do you have any idea of what will happen next?" he asks.

I shake my head. "I'm not sure, but I think that the elves are going to try to train me. You saw what happened when I tried to do it on my own. I don't even know how it happened. It felt like every ounce of energy in my body fell away."

"Well then, who do we ask to find out what to do, oh mighty chosen one?" Taytra says mockingly.

"Me," Moraine says stepping into the room.

"Oh great," she mumbles under her breath, but after a look from Father, she says no more.

"Your Majesty, how are you?" I ask politely.

"Me? I should be asking you that. I wasn't the one who tried to cast spells without training."

"But I didn't mean to do it! It just happened, I don't even know *how* I did it," I say defensively.

"So she will be trained?" Father asks, cutting in. "How will she be trained? No one else can do this right?"

"It will be difficult, there were very few benders left after the wars but, we have information to give her. Before we get to that, we have to finish the ceremony." She must have seen the surprise on my face. "Not to worry Shauna, this portion is in secret." She turns to my father and sister. "Jamie, Taytra, this is between the two of us. I will ask you to remain in the hallway. You can come back in when this is finished."

"What are you going to do to my sister? She doesn't have to do anything she doesn't want to," Taytra says furiously.

"Tay! Please calm down."

"Shauna is right, Taytra you must calm down. You saw what happened at the first ceremony. Unless we complete it with this one, that will happen any time Shauna uses her powers, and that would put her in a lot of danger. This will help her body adapt to the changes happening to her," the queen says.

"Tay I will still be the same person. Even if I act differently, I will always be your sister."

Taytra shakes her head and leaves the room.

"Tay!"

She turns back, tears in the corners of her eyes.

"I love you." I whisper.

"I love you too," Taytra whispers and heads out the door, My father nods to me and to Moraine before he leaves to try to comfort her.

* * *

Taytra flies from the room. Her knuckles turn white as she clutches the red fabric of her dress. "Who does she think she is?" She lets her back thud against the wall, ignoring the dull pain that comes with it, she slides to the floor. The stone is cold beneath her fingers, but it isn't enough to cool the anger in her chest.

Her father follows behind slowly closing the door behind him. "She is just trying to protect us," he says gently.

"No," she snaps. "She is trying to take my sister away from us." Taytra runs a hand over her face trying to keep her voice from shaking. "Father, why is this happening?" Taytra asks when he sits down beside her. "First Mother, now this queen is trying to force Shauna to leave us?"

Jamie slides down to sit beside his daughter. "Tay, you know

Shauna isn't trying to shove you out. She doesn't think she is better than you now." Taytra shrugs. "Look at what happened yesterday. You had to stab someone to protect all of us. She is in a dangerous situation. The last thing she needs is her family fighting."

Taytra looks at her hands. "She is my little sister, I had to protect her. What else was I supposed to do? I'm not sorry I did it."

He sighs and pulls her close so her head lies on his shoulder. She takes a deep, steadying breath.

"I know my dear, and I wouldn't think of it any other way. You will still be my daughter. I will always be Shauna's father. You will still be her big sister".

"You make it sound like she is dead," Taytra says pulling away from her father.

"I'm sorry, I don't mean to. It's just you saw what happened last night. I think the Queen is right in some regards. She doesn't want us to be used against Shauna, or us to be hurt because of her."

"If not for us, for me, she would be dead! She needs us!"

"You may be right. But for now, this is what she needs us to do, she needs to focus on herself and this magick that's inside her, and grow strong, so she can fight and be whatever a Fritual is." Taytra makes a sound that is a combination of a sigh and a growl, Shauna hadn't been faking those tears last night. Pushing her family away was the last thing she wanted to do.

Taytra lets her head fall back on her father's shoulder. "She needs us. She knows that she needs us," she says in quiet defiance.

"She does," he says quietly, and something in it makes Taytra look up at her father. He swallows a few times, his face flushed. He wouldn't look at her. "But I think she also knows that this is something we can't be with her for, we have to support from afar. She is going to change and she—"

"I don't want her to change," Taytra snaps pushing up and away from her father. "I know I sound like a child. But I don't want her to change. I don't want our family to change. So much has already happened, and I don't want to go through it again." She clutches at her skirt stomping across the floor trying to get some of her pent-up anger to just flow out of her feet and into the floor with each thud. She stomped one last time, and it felt like the ground shifted slightly under her feet. "Did you?" There was a soft rumbling of stamping feet moving through the halls. Taytra, slightly unnerved, moved to the wall peering out the window.

Her father didn't follow her. He was used to Taytra needing to step away and cool down. She took several deep breaths looking out into the world she had known. But it looked different out there. It was only noon, but it looked like twilight. The sky was dark and black fog swirled all around. "Father come here," she said warily.

"What is it, Tay?" he asks.

"Why is that fog black? Fog isn't normally black," she said. She knew she sounded a bit childish, but the dark, swirling clouds were unnerving.

Jamie pushes himself up with a small grunt and joined her at the window. She felt her father tense beside her. "Come on, we need to tell someone about this." He glances at the door where Moraine and Shauna are finishing the ceremony. "We need to get help, we need to get the guards."

"The Queen!"

53

"No, she is busy with your sister we can't interrupt them we need to find the guards let's go! We need to warn them!"

"But Shauna?"

"Come on." He grabs her elbow and drags her down the hall, glancing over his shoulder at the door. "I know, but we need to let them finish the ceremony."

"See this is why she needs us— we are always protecting her," Taytra grumbles under her breath.

Jamie glares at his daughter's back, but she care or notice as she walks down the hall ahead of her father.

She scans all the side passages until she sees a guard making his way rather slowly down the corridor. "Hello!" she calls rushing up to him. "Hey!" she calls again when he didn't respond. "Hello! I'm talking to you," her annoyance barely withheld.

The guard turned to her slowly, his movements tight like ropes were attached to his limbs pulling his every move. He leers at her, his eyes taking in every inch of her from her rumpled skirt to her fluffy hair. "What do you want human?" he asks, clipping off the ends of his words.

"I— uh help, help, I wanted help," Taytra says trying to keep calm while she took several steps back. Her eyes locked on this elf's eyes, his pupils have blown out like he had no irises, just flat black disks. "But I see that you are busy, so we will just leave you be," Taytra said trying to wave her father back.

Jamie not seeing Taytra's unease keeps coming around the corner. "Oh good sir, I am glad we found you we—"

"We're just leaving," Taytra cut in, grabbing her father's elbow. "We were just leaving," she repeats trying to tug him down the hall. "His eyes," she hisses, a smile plastered on her face, "look at his eyes. Someone's used magick on him."

Jamie looks at the elf and nods. "She is right, we will be going."

"No, no I don't think you will. I have to take you to the cells."

A nervous giggle escapes from Taytra's lips before she can reign it in. "Right the cells. You see I have this meeting today and I promised them that you know I wouldn't miss it because I was trapped in the cells. So I really should be going."

"I am sorry. But you will miss your meeting." The guard reaches out and grabs Jamie's other arm.

"No," he growls trying to pull away. "Tay, go run!" he says and pushes her away from him.

Taytra who wasn't expecting to be pushed, stumbles, her foot catching in her dress. She tumbles to the ground smacking her knee on the uneven floor, pain swelling around her knee.

"Father," she cries as she struggles to her feet her knee feeling hot and tight already.

"Tay, go, I'll stall him," Jamie say twisting and turning, trying to get an arm free to lash out at the elf.

Taytra takes the first step away then another. "God damn it, Shauna," she growls pushing herself around the corner.

She hears her father struggling with the guard as she hobbles away. *Go, Damn it go!* She thinks. She knows that though he means well her father can't hold off the guard for long. He is just a human and the guard is an elf.

10

The Sisters

"Great," I say letting the tears fall freely. "I am supposedly the descendent of some great elf, and here I am a blubbering fool."

Moraine hands me a handkerchief. "Shauna, you are fine. You have been through a lot in the last twenty-four hours and no one can blame you for it. Least of all your family." She smiles at me and part of me wants to snap, I don't want her sympathy. "Now let's begin."

I can't think though. My mind is blank, words don't want to form in my mouth, I just feel a swirling pit of emotions in my stomach: fear, rage, eagerness, defeat. *But you want me to make them leave.*

From her sleeve, she pulls a book. On the cover, it says 'Fritual Ka Aka' which in elven meant 'chosen of the water.'

"What is this?" I ask trying to make out the authors name.

"It is a spell book; I will warn you it is written entirely in Elven," Moraine says. "The last of our water benders gathered together to create this book in the case that none of them were alive when you were named."

"Oh," I say. It is slowly dawning on me how long these

people have waited for me. "Ok, then can I have some sort of dictionary? My Elven isn't that great right now. I stopped my elven lessons two summers ago," I say flipping through the book recognizing some phases and not knowing where to start with others.

"Of course, now flip to page five," she says. "You should see something that says 'Aken tes wentes.'"

I nod. "Got it." I scan the page trying to translate the complex text.

"Let me see, yes, this is the spell that will complete your ceremony," Moraine says running a hand along the text.

"Please excuse my asking, but can you explain the Royal Magick? They couldn't or wouldn't in my lessons."

"Yes, I am a spell caster. There are a few of us left though we tend to keep that side of our lives to ourselves. Every ruler is able to do some two forms of magick up to a certain point. I can cast minor water and spirit magick spells. Many consider my abilities weak. But I was the third child of a king. None of the schoolmasters my father hired deemed it important because none of them thought I would rule. But over the years I have done a lot of my own education. Shall we begin?" she asks, and I nod.

Moraine glances at the book then begins tracing lines on my face as she speaks the ancient words "'Terris, Apeito, Aka, Fugaste, Akasa. Aka simpore baka timpto falan skikto atonake. Floodo pawtora costana.' Earth, air, water, fire, and spirit. Water is peaceful; it floods the rivers and the lakes. 'Bunaro back tarse lavente weing stark fathor.' We thank water for the sweet drink to quench thy thirst. 'Andre bunaraa backtares aka taka aka fritual ta gevive aka' and we are grateful to the water giving power to the water Savior bless this child with thine power."

There is a soft blue glow emanating from her fingers as Moraine brushes my face and neck, the skin tingling under her touch. Her voice grows more intense and powerful as the spell progresses. Her voice falls away leaving the air buzzing with energy. A chill runs up my spine, sending shivers down my arms and legs.

"There, that should do it," she says with a sigh, sitting back slightly. She keeps glancing up at my face but not looking me in the eye then down at the book again.

She does it two more times before I gather the courage to ask, "Moraine is something wrong?"

"Wrong?" she says distractedly. "Oh no nothing is wrong per say, it's just well it never mentioned this." She thumbs through the pages looking for a specific passage. "Ah, here it is. Right, I well— look." She holds up a mirror that lies on the bedside table.

What the book hadn't mentioned at first was a series of intricate spiral glowing blue cascading down my face like water. The spot feels cool to the touch and slightly raised like a tattoo. "It is beautiful, I would never have expected this — but Moraine how am I supposed to hide now? It's like a warning sign 'oh look here I come! I am the water Fritual come get me.'" Moraine looks so torn-up about it; I realize then the pressure she must feel. I am the blessed one who is supposed to protect her people. But, things haven't been going well so far. "Moraine, don't worry we will figure it out it's just a matter of time."

"The book says it will only appear when you cast magick. So as long as you don't cast you will be hidden." Her voice falters as a deep rumbling echoes off the walls then falls silent before a massive crash. We look at each other and rush into the hall.

Guards rush to and fro as we stand there. "Come on!" We take off running. We stop when we run into one of the captains. Trying to catch her breathe Moraine asks "sir, what is going on."

"Your majesty, the Dark Ones are at the wall. We are holding them off as best as we can, but it won't last long. Some of them are already inside the wall; they have control over some of the guards. Lady Shauna I would suggest you run."

"Run? I can't run! Where is my family?"

"Thank you, Captain, Shauna let's go!" And she pulls me away running to her rooms.

* * *

Tay finds a door and bursts into it hoping that she won't find something or someone who isn't friendly on the other side. The room is dark, dusty, but thankfully empty. She leans against the back of the door, breathing hard through the pain radiating from her leg. "You're such a baby," she growls to herself. She clenches her jaw, bending her knee over and over so it won't get stiff. "Okay, let's see what I can find," she glances around the room and limps over to the window. Taytra slowly peels back the curtain hoping no one is on the other side. The black landscape doesn't look inviting but there isn't anyone on the other side to greet her, friend or foe. The curtain is made of a heavy dark navy, in the dim light, it looks almost black. "You could be useful," she says yanking it down with a clatter.

She looks from the curtain to the top of the window. "That was stupid," she scolds herself, rushing to stand behind the door, clutching the musty curtain to her chest.

She waits with bated breath for one hundred rapid heartbeats. She keeps her eyes trained on the floor near the door. Waiting for a shadow to pass by. When she feels her heart beat slow, and nothing walks past, she slowly moves to wrap the curtain around her shoulders. It doesn't quite work as a cloak, but she could pull it over her head to hide her face. With one hand clasping the fabric around her throat, Taytra reaches for the door. The handle creaks under her hand, and the door lets out a moan of disuse that she didn't noticed in her rush to get inside. With the door open a crack she peeks out. One of her now frizzy curls falls over her shoulder, and she tucks it away again so she can see to her right. The way is clear. Taytra moves out into the corridor. A bead of cold sweat drips down the side of her neck. She stares hard at the flagstones at her feet, she wants to run, to run as quickly as she can and to just get out of here. But a somewhat more sensible part of her tells her that running would draw more attention to herself than she wants. So she walks, one step at a time, trying to look like everything is normal. Like the world isn't falling apart around her.

She pauses at a window trying to determine where exactly she is in the castle. She doesn't know her way around this massive labyrinth. The first step is to get to the ground floor or find someone who isn't under Dark One control. She would take either one.

The night before when Shauna had passed out, and the elves had carried her off, they had left Taytra and Father in the hall. Taytra had used that time to berate the guard in charge of them. When they were finally taken half an hour later to get a change of clothes, her demands to be with Shauna were eventually given traction. They were taken up the stairs straight to the infirmary where Taytra had fallen asleep, her head on her sister's bed.

Father had gone to explore while she slept. He was stir-crazy.

The times when he could stay still as a statue had died with their mother.

Taytra continues down the hall. She peers into every open doorway. She can't help it. The empty space draws her in. But even as it draws her in each doorway makes her pause for a heartbeat. Her footsteps reverberate, letting all who may be near know exactly where she is. She flattens herself against the wall. What she wouldn't give for a good pair of pair of pants at the moment. She cranes her neck around the corner and swiftly pulls it back when she sees movement. *Damn it,* she thinks. She tries to move as quickly as she can back down the hall to an open doorway. The knob clanks under her hand and does not open. She tries again. "Come on," Taytra mutters under her breath.

"You there, Dark One," the guard yells, his voice accompanied by the sound of metal scraping. He has drawn his sword and brought it up in front of himself ready to use it.

Taytra steps out of the shadows and flings away her makeshift cloak. "Relax friend," she says putting out a hand of encouragement, trying to get the guard to lower the blade. "I am no Dark One."

"Lady Shauna I apologize let's get you—"

"I am Taytra," Taytra interrupts. "I am not Lady Shauna, I am her sister. She is still with Queen Moraine in the infirmary. The Dark Ones have taken our father, we need to get help."

The guard takes a moment processing the change in his stance toward her. Would he still protect her even if she wasn't the Fritual? "Lady Taytra, right now we need to get more guards. There aren't many of us, but we need to keep you safe. You may be needed."

Taytra follows, jogging to keep up with the man's longer

stride. "Needed? What do you mean?"

"Queen Moraine told us last night that if the castle were to fall to the Dark Ones, we would need to get Lady Shauna out of here. You, Lady Taytra may be needed to play a decoy," he turns to her, a sort of sad look on his face. "You know you look like her, you two could be twins." He looks sorry that this is their only solution, but has to follow his orders all the same.

"Yes, yes I know. Tell me what needs to be done."

11

Shuana

"**M**oraine! Stop! Where is my sister and father?" I stop outside the door to her rooms demanding answers.

"I don't know, I don't know where your family is, but I will tell them where you have gone. We have to get you to safety."

"Gone? What are you talking about? I can't leave now."

"You must leave. We cannot hold the castle." She glances outside at the swirl of black magick. "It looks like they are here in force. I will give you the books and foods and a weapon, but then you have to go! Come on." She drags me to her room shoving books into a bag and throwing a dark cloak over my shoulders. She gives me a dagger and a short sword that I have no clue how to use. Then cloaked and armed we make for the kitchen. When the bag is filled with food, she brings me to a statue of an elf in a scholar's robes. Moraine reaches down and twists the right foot, and a passage opens up behind the figure.

"Moraine I'm so sorry. If it weren't for me nothing like this would ever happen. Your palace and... I am so sorry," I say standing in the doorway.

"My castle can be rebuilt, you cannot. I would rather know

you were safely away from this danger than have a big castle anyway." She kisses me on the forehead then says gravely, "Go with my blessing, find the other Frituals, you can't fight alone. Find them and band together. Grow strong, become a force to be reckoned with. Then come home. Save your people. Save your family. Be safe." She wants to say more but when we hear the sound of pounding feet shoves me into the tunnel and closes the passage.

I pull the hood up higher over my face and move through the darkness, pausing to let my eyes adjust to the gloom.

Things could have been better. I think *Here I am running for my life, when I'm supposed to be* so *powerful,* but I don't know how to access that power. I have a weapon that I don't know how to use and a week's worth of food. *It could be worse, you could be captured or dead* I think trying to stay on the bright side of this literally dark situation. Every thirty feet or so a hole is in the ceiling casting dim light. Looking up through the first I see the sky was growing darker by the moment.

Move now I tell myself, I sure am not going to get stuck here in this false night, in the dark, feeling my way through a secret passage where no one would be able to come find me.

At first, I walk quickly, but as it grows dimmer and dimmer, I speed up. The cloak tangles about my ankles causing me to stumble. With every passing moment, the pack gets heavier and heavier. I have to stop to take breaks more often as time goes by. I am not used to having to run for my life that is for sure.

"Shauna? Are you there?" a voice calls from the darkness.

"Who's there?" I snap, pulling out the dagger. I wince at the slight echo as my voice bounces off the cave walls. *Stupid! You just gave yourself away!* I am not ready to fight, but I will try. I turn the blade over and over in my hand trying to get a good grip on it, but my finger are slick with sweat.

"Hurry Damian knows you are in the tunnel, his men will be through soon," the voice said.

"Damian? Damian's dead," I say, fear letting the words escape.

I creep forward trying to see who it is, it sounds like Taytra but it could be a Dark One. I squeal and launch myself at her when I turn the corner and see who it is. "Tay! You're safe!" It is her, hair in a braid hanging down, red dress, now with a curtain hanging around her shoulders? I can see the loops where the pole would have hung from the fabric. "You look interesting?" I say squeezing her to me.

I can tell she is trying not to laugh as she says, "Of course it's me who else would it be?" We break apart, and the smile fades. "What is that on your face?"

I touch the edge of the mark. "This was the final ceremony, it marked me as the Fritual. Can you see it with the hood up?" I bring my hood up again.

"I can't see the markings, but Shauna I can see a glow." She looks away. "We're so different now."

"Tay we aren't. We are the same people- it's just different circumstances." Down the passageway ever so faintly I can hear the heavy tramp of feet. "Do you hear that?"

"What am I listening for exactly?" she asks listening hard.

"You can't hear that?" I ask. The footsteps are getting louder.

"I am practically blind right now I only saw you cause of your face," she says still straining to hear.

I can see everything around me. *Did the ceremony heighten my senses too? How did I miss that before?* I wonder but think it's better to keep this thought to myself.

65

"So what is it? Feet or something?"

I nod.

"Okay switch dresses with me I will lead them the other way, so you can run!"

"What? No!"

"Come on we don't really have any other options now do we? We can't let them catch you."

"Tay where is Father?" I ask as she does the buttons on the back of my dress.

"I was able to hide before they saw me but they got him. Don't even think of playing the hero. You need to leave."

"Who said I was?" I ask trying to hide the fact that, that was indeed what I had been thinking.

"Please, I am your sister remember. I know you."

I sigh and pull the cloak back on. *Of course, she would be able to tell.*

She leads me to the edge of the passage where it opens up onto the forest. We hold our breath as a stick snaps too close for comfort. I signal to her that I will be going to the left. She nods and gives my hand a squeeze before beginning to thunder her way through the woods making as much noise as possible to pull the men in that direction.

When she has gone, I make my way through the trees as silently as I can.

12

Taytra

Taytra glances over her shoulder pleased to see that her sister has already disappeared into the false night. Shauna has always been good at that.

Taytra thuds through the forest 'careful' to grab branches and pull them back as she runs, so they snap back against the others. The branches reach out and grab at the sheer material of her dress. The bark turns her hands red as her hands slip on one large branch, it snaps back clawing at her face. "Damn it." She crouches low to the ground to get away, the finger-like twigs dragging several red lines across her face.

Shauna, this better be worth it she thinks, crawling kicking logs out of the way. Taytra pauses under one tree and reaches down to the bottom of the dress gripping the hem of the fabric she rips it from the hem to her thigh. Hopefully, she would be able to move a bit more freely now. Her knee hurts. She parts the fabric letting the swollen and bruised skin pop out. It is starting to become stiff. Each time she moves it, it feels like little needles are spreading out from her knee. Then there is the bruising, the fall hadn't hurt that much at the moment, but then again she had been trying to run away from an elf who was possessed by dark magick. She probably just didn't notice. Now the bruising is spreading all around her kneecap, distorted by the swelling. She shifts her weight to her hands and works her way back up into a standing position, groaning as she puts pressure on her leg. "Let's go," she tells herself aloud, clenching her teeth against the hot pain as she takes a few steps. "I need to move. Stopping makes it stiffer."

She can see the tall spires of the castle between the trees. One tower toward the west doesn't look like the gleaming marble beauty it had been the day before. Now it stands sentinel in a seething black fog. It steams out, spinning its arms reaching farther and farther out over the city covering it a blanket of darkness. Her heart pounds faster as one particular cloud of black smoke lifts away from the growing mass. She watches feeling the air around her grow cold, the plants, shriveling in a sudden frost. Taytra crouches low again, sticks and rocks digging into her hands, pricking into her feet.

When had she lost her left shoe? It doesn't matter now.

The black cloud is shrinking morphing into something else. Growing ever closer. She takes a deep breath, trying to fill her lungs and soothe her pounding heart. *What is that thing?* She glances around as the dark shadows around her grow deeper and deeper, their contents becoming less clear. "This is fine; we are fine, its just dark magick, who cares right?" she says trying to talk herself down, but her voice cracks, the sound stark against the silence that hangs around her. "I am Shauna Flynn," Taytra whispers drawing the darkness closer to her. "I am a Fritual. I am Shauna Flynn. They will want you alive. Right?" She glances up at the magick. It is like a predator stalking her through the trees.

Stories from her childhood ring loud in her head. Elves angry at the race of man, killing them for sport. Razing the land with black fire. Were all those stories just Dark Ones, masquerading as good elves? Like Damian who had been hiding as a Dark One for years and years.

She hears a hissing noise as the black magick comes closer, her heart is like a jack rabbit's, pounding a thousand beats a minute. "I can't stay here. I can't stay here," she repeats into the darkness. She jumps to her feet, wincing as she comes back down on to her knee. She crashes through the trees moving as quickly and as loudly as she can. The magick knows where she is. She doesn't understand how it can track her, but every time she glances over her shoulder she sees it right there on her tail. Taytra wants them to find her, just wait till they do. They will be in for a surprise.

Run Shauna run! Get away from here; she wills to her sister.

It isn't long before she is out of breath, and stumbling more than running, her knee is getting so stiff. She pauses for half a second and picks up a large branch, using it to help support her weight. She knows it won't be much longer until they catch her. The dark hissing noise grows louder and louder. "Come to usssss we will bring you no harrrmmmmm. Come now, your family will be saffffffe."

"Never!" she shouts and hobbles faster.

The voices close in more and more as she slows down. She stumbles onto a game trail and decides this was where she would take her stand. She swings the branch, and it passes straight through shifting the magick like mist. It feels oddly warm as it creeps up her arm across her skin. She smacks at it turning her skin red. "Get off of me!" she snaps, swinging the branch again not realizing how close she is, she strikes a tree. A buzzing pain runs up her arms numbing her hands.

"Commmmee withhh ussss," it hisses again loud in her ears blocking out every sound.

She tries to hold her breath as it wraps up around her head. It makes her dizzy; the world is flashing from light to dark. She falls to her knees, but she doesn't feel the pain this time. She makes it out of the smoke cloud for a second before it drops on her, pressing in her nose and mouth. The smoke clears for a moment, and Damian steps through the swirling tendrils.

Taytra's eyes widen in fear. This man was dead; she had killed him! His black shirt gapes in the front, and she catches a glimpse of the hole in his chest and neck where she had stabbed him. She manages a weak "Run Shauna!" before all is smoke and blackness.

13

Shauna

I sneak through the shadows created by the Dark Ones magick moving in a direction I hope is away from danger. My mind is on a looped track, repeating the same questions over and over, *Is Taytra ok? Is Father okay? What will Moraine do? Can I ever come home? How long will I be safe?*

I heard when it caught Taytra. The thing that thought it was hunting me through the woods. With the noise, she was making it didn't take long to find her. I knew she was trying to get caught, I knew she would kill me if I even took one step back toward the castle but I still wanted to turn back and help her. She tried to fight, but they quickly overtook her. I heard her fighting, then the silence. I didn't even hear them pursuing her. Only silence. That's what pushed me on. I had no way of knowing how close they- or- it was to me.

Now I am on my own. They have to know she wasn't the one they were looking for. So the hunt for me is on. My limbs feel like sacks of grain hanging off me; I just want to stop. But If I do, I am done for.

I don't know how far into the forest I am, or where exactly to turn. I used to go into the woods on my side of the lake all the time, but I had no reason to ever be on this side of the lake.

Philippe used to sneak into our barn and angle himself so he could reflect light off of a mirror and into my room. Some days Taytra would notice it and would tear the place apart looking for its source. It would take me a bit, but once I had distracted her, I would sneak out and meet him outside. We always had a good laugh about it. But we were always back before sunset. I had heard the stories of course. "Shauna, you have a wild imagination." Philippe said when I had asked him. But he had heard the stories too. He carried his knife the next time we went out.

The forest behind my house was young, soft and comforting. This one is the opposite. The trees are closer together, the shadows deeper. I move in the shadows, using them to hide from whatever prying eyes may watch my movements. But I long to be free of the shadows that make my skin crawl. I can't imagine how dark it must be to any "normal" human. Because even now I know I am now different. It must have been so dark for Taytra. This red dress of hers is all I have to remind me of my family. Drenched in sweat, torn, and muddy. If she ever saw what I had done to her favorite dress, she would kill me herself.

An owl hoots near me, and I nearly jump out of my skin. It has grown dark enough to confuse the creatures of the night.

When I see the moon illuminating the sky, I know I have finally crossed out of the dark magick. I am exhausted. The cuts on my ankles have stopped bleeding but still sting. My face feels raw from wiping the sweat off my face. The hand holding my knife is cramped up again. Slowly as I move in a direction that I hope is a straight line, the trees around me begin to thin. "I have to stop somewhere," I murmur to myself. My chest hurts from moving fast and breathing hard. Looking far ahead, I can see the edge of the woods. Beyond it a vast open plain of tall grass and wild flowers. I can't cross a plain now. It would be too open, and I am too tired. I lean against a tree, trying to get a small amount of strength to get a "safe" place to sleep. I push off the tree and feel a few new scrapes get added to my hands. I find a small clearing with a large tree in the center, its branches reaching to the sky. Another tree has fallen on it, and over time, the two have formed a small alcove. For some reason seeing all the branches and roots weaving together makes me feel more comfortable and safe. I collapse just in front of the opening. I lie down pressing my flushed face into the cool, soft dirt.

I lie there savoring the moments of peace when I hear someone approaching. Fear clutches at my heart anew. *They found me, they found me, they found me*, my thoughts scream at me. As quietly as I can, I shove the bag behind me and tuck myself in with it. I wipe my hands of the sweat collecting in my hands, gripping the dagger hard. I pull the hood of my cloak high to hide my face and close my eyes praying they can't see me. If I can't see them, they can't see me right? Is this the end? I can't help thinking *I'm sorry Moraine I tried to get away but, I'm am going to fight I'm not going down without a fight.*

The voice calls something out in Elven. I try to translate it, but in my panic, all the words I know are gone. "Who's there?" they call again, this time in the language of man. His voice from the edge of the clearing. My body tenses in fear, but I don't reply. "I know you are there, so you might as well come out." The voice is closer this time. "Come on now, I won't hurt you. What are you running from?" Again I don't respond, I don't dare uncover my face. Taytra said she could see it. "Alright, you asked for it. Blackractaz!" The voice says something I didn't understand in Elven; then I am moving.

The roots that had protected me are moving away, filling the air around me with soft moonlight. I snap my eyes open when a vine suddenly wraps itself around my ankle dragging me out further into the clearing. I hack at it with the dagger, but another root comes and pulls my hand above my head. I twist my wrist trying to cut at the root. I watch helplessly as my bag zooms across into the woods. Vines are inching up my legs and around my waist hoisting me into the air. I twist and begin to bite desperately at one. But then one is around my neck turning my head forward. The thin vines crawl up my face entangling themselves in my hair and holding me still. I want nothing more than to scream, but if this isn't a Dark One then it would alert them to where I am. Just when I think I am going to pass out from lack of air and my sight goes fuzzy the voice says, "Moviataca," and the vines around my neck loosen and fall away. A single vine comes up and pushes the hood from my face.

An elf comes through the trees, in his hand is my book, my Fritual book. His face is like mine, but the lines are harsher, like mountains and rocks, or the claw of a bear, slim vines wrapping it all glowing in a deep forest green. The green glowing coming off his skin, just like the blue glow that came off my own. I cough and hack as I am lowered to the ground, where my legs give out sending me wheezing and lightheaded to the dirt.

"Who are you?" I wheeze clutching my throat and coughing.

"A friend, come on we need to move." He hauls me to my feet and hands me back my stuff.

"Friend?" I wheeze. "The friends I know don't try to kill me." I say grabbing my knife off the ground.

My world tilts, and he grabs my arm. I jump and swing the knife at his hand, but a vine comes up and catches my hand. "Look they are close we need to get into hiding. Better than your idea of hiding at least."

I glare at him, hiding my fear. *Tay always hides behind the wall of fiery rebuttals why shouldn't I?* But I follow him, clutching the bag to my chest and holding the blade out in front of me. He leads me to a tree stump, glanced around him before muttering something and the roots move, opening and stretching, revealing a hole and a ladder. I follow him down, and the roots close up around my head concealing us completely. I turn in wonder at the perfect little cave he has here.

It has to be twenty feet in diameter. A small fire crackles in the center, and the smell of roasting meat makes my mouth water. Only then do I realize how hungry I am. He goes to the fire and turns the food on the spit. "Are you hungry?" he asks, not trying to make me do anything, as I stand close to the exit of the tree cave. I feel equal parts safe and like a caged animal.

"Um yes, but I have food if it would—" I stammer.

"Here," he says handing me the stick "Careful you don't want to burn yourself." He holds the stick out to me and grins as I tentatively grab it before tearing into the meat.

"Thanks," I say through a mouthful of food.

"You're welcome; I guess I owe you after, well you know."

"Almost choking me to death? Dragging me out of hiding?" I snap, my head still pounded from the lack of air. The headache would probably last the night.

"Well yeah." He sounds genuinely ashamed of doing that. "I really am sorry, but I couldn't be sure that, you weren't the enemy. You had your face covered and all so I couldn't tell whether or not you were a Dark One. But then the book," he pauses slowing the avalanche of words with a breath. "I am Paulo," He said putting out a hand "I guess that you know who I am, now at least. I am the Fritual ka Apeito. The earth Fritual."

I nod shaking his hand "I understand, just a little shocked and worn out. My name is Shauna, I am the Fritual ka Aka. That is, I'm water I was just — just, would discover be the right word? Oh well, I was just discovered last night." It has been the longest day of my life that was for sure. I know I have to trust him; he is in the same boat. So I explain everything that had happened in the last twenty-four hours. "I honestly can't believe that I found someone this fast! Well, you found me I guess, but you know what I mean."

"I'm surprised too. I have been here for about three months."

"And nobody knew you were here?"

"No, there is a spell I put in this area this looks like a two-year-old sapling to anyone who I don't bring in. The Dark Ones have started to gather on the plain about half a mile from here. I couldn't figure out why. Now I know." He pauses looking at me for a moment, then to his hands. "I'm sorry about what just happened out there. I want to tell you what happened to me so that you can trust me." I nod and sit down near the fire trying to relax as Paulo's words flow over me. "I took my test again two years ago. I was as you said, discovered. I took it when I was one hundred like all elves, but somethings started to happen so I was asked to take it again. I was lucky in the fact that it took a little longer for the Dark Ones to infiltrate our castle. The King told me with his last dying breaths to go into hiding. There isn't anything left there for me. When I wouldn't come out of hiding, they killed my brother, the only family I had left." He pauses thinking of it before going on. "I never thought to look for the others because I didn't hear anything about the other Frituals."

"I think the Dark Ones are putting out false reports. The last I heard was that Gradtadia was doing amazing in trade," I say, but even as the words escape my lips, I can hear the lies in them.

He laughed humorlessly. "Oh how I wish I could tell you that was the truth. The city has never been in more danger than now. Sickness and starvation are everywhere. The Dark Ones killed all the crops we had harvested and burned all the fields. I am surprised that some of the other kingdoms haven't heard yet, I guess it is too early in the season for food shortages. Anyway, I stayed around for a year, I was helping, and trying to help get the crops to grow but I was almost caught too many times, so I had to leave." The pain in his voice is palpable. He felt he had given up on his people.

"Well, we are both alone, can we be alone together? Will you help me so we can restore our people and our cities?" I offer, putting the now empty skewer at my side. The statement sounds so bright, and grand, inspirational even, but here we are sitting alone and scared in a magick tree cave.

"I will gladly help you bring them down," he says resolutely. "Only thing is we can't do this just the two of us you know."

"Oh no, our first task is to find the other Frituals and to train. Then – well, we will have to wait to see what happens." I say hearing the echo of Moraine's words in them. "While we're here, do you want to tell me about home? I've never heard anything about the plateau beside that it's a beautiful place."

He spent a second thinking. "Well, a more beautiful place I've never seen. Sweeping green fields, waist-high wildflowers in every color you can think of. The sun would shine through the stain glass windows painting an array of colors all over the floor. The king's throne wasn't made of precious metals like gold, but it was made of the King's favorite wood. It was a solid piece of maple that a master carpenter made during the first four years of the king's reign. In the end, it didn't look like a throne but a mass of vines. But looks can be deceiving." His eyes clouded over as he thought about his past. "We held my ceremony there. There wasn't a place to move the room was packed, and I was so nervous. I didn't know what to expect. But it was beautiful. I was called onto the stage, and they named me the one. And there was such a cheer. I never felt prouder in my life.

"Behind the throne, there was a large stained-glass window depicting scenes from nature. They had me recite the words in the elven tongue and the sun shone through the window casting its rays onto my face. Where the light touched, this formed." He pauses and points to the marks on his face. Then sadness falls like a veil over him. "Then a few weeks later just when I was starting to get good at the training. The King's Head Guard stabbed him in his sleep and then came to my chamber. The rest you already know. I ran, I hid, I ended up here. Then I found you."

"Your ceremony was so different from mine," I say in shock, picturing the lines on his face, unlike Moraine's soft fingers tracing my skin.

Soon after we finish eating, we head to bed. I am exhausted from my flight and the events at the palace, so it doesn't take me long to fall asleep.

14

Moraine

Moraine was not new to war. It was a constant theme in her rule. From the first war that her sister started, to the second war with man, and the rebellions that came just about every century.

Moraine the Rabble Rouser. Moraine the Peace-bringer. To some, Moraine the Breaker of Vows. She regretted some of the decisions she had made over the centuries. But there was none she regretted more than letting Damian stay as the leader of her high guard. One could see that in the small gestures the Queen made trapped in her cell. Her shoulders were slumped, and she didn't sit nearly as tall as she usually did. She had done her duty. She had found the Fritual of Cabineral lake, she had completed all of her jobs as queen to find them and name them, and she had even gone as far as to plan how to get them out of the city. They always had a plan for what to do if they were attacked from outside the city walls. But, they never made a plan for what to do if they were attacked from the inside.

They had been taken by their own men. Men they now knew who had been controlled by Damian, to the dungeons. The dark cells that had stayed empty for nearly a hundred and fifty years.

Moraine believed in justice, but a justice that wasn't cruel. It was a system that let her people be held more accountable and let the dungeons cells remain empty.

They had tied her hands behind her back, ripping the fabric from the sleeves of her ceremonial gown. They made her stand and watch as the citizens of her city who resisted, and the men and women who had not gone back to the human town were escorted through the halls. Children were screaming, and mothers were crying. Husbands and older sons glared at her, and not for the first time she felt that looks could kill.

They put her in the cell next to Jamie and Taytra. Taytra was in the corner. Moraine couldn't tell if she was crying because she was scared or because she was angry. From what she knew of the girl, it was probably a mixture of the two.

Jamie who was the first to be brought down to these deeper cells is sitting across the cell from his daughter. His lip is split, and he has bruises blooming on his arms where he had fought against his captor. He occasionally gets up and paces the cell. Each time he rises his movements are stiff, but slowly pacing the small area he is able to loosen his muscles.

It is damp and cold below the castle. The windows are small slits high up on the wall that let in barely any light. It is the perfect cell. Moraine just never thought she would be the one behind bars.

"What happens now?" Taytra asks from the cell next door. She, while looking pale and mentally drained, doesn't look to badly hurt. Her knee is bruised and she has lots of scratches. But nothing created by her capture.

"We lie low," her father replies.

Taytra scoffs. "Well I guess it's a good thing we are in the dungeons then huh. We can't lie any lower."

Straw rustles, and her father reaches over to her. "Look the situation isn't great. But we don't have a choice now, do we? We just need to—"

"We just do what? We can't do anything down here can we? We can't help Shauna, we can't do anything," she snaps pulling away from him. "You! You took Shauna. You could do some magick- do something! Get us out of here," she says rounding on the queen.

"Tay she is a queen, you can't speak to her like that."

"She doesn't look much like a queen now does she? She is just like us, locked up in a cell underground!"

"Come on Tay."

"It's alright Jamie, she is right," Moraine says sitting up, and straightening her skirts slightly. She has a job, a purpose, calming her subject. "She is right, we are in a bad situation right now, and there isn't much we can do. To answer you, I can't do any magick right now, and if I do those who have imprisoned us will know." Moraine points to a shimmering black disk on the door of each cell. "See that? It is a type of alarm."

"Does that stop any tampering of the locks?" Jamie asks moving to look at the lock.

"I have heard of some that have that ability, the only way to test it would be to try to play with it," Moraine says. "I feel like if any of us were to touch the locks, then we would set off the alarms as well. But again, the only way to know would be to test it."

"And you don't suggest that," Taytra says reading the look on the queen's face.

"No, I wouldn't."

"So now we should do what then?" Jamie asks settling back

down in his corner.

"Now, we wait."

Taytra pinches up her face in exasperation. "And what exactly do you expect us to wait for?" she asks. "Huh, what the hell could sitting here, in a cold dungeon do to help us?"

Moraine pauses, planning out her answer before speaking. This is not a crowd of elves who had known her for years. It isn't people that would trust her words and accept any plans she had created. No, this is a scared human girl, who looks at her and sees the person that took away her sister. She doesn't know Moraine and has every reason in the book to hate her right now. "We wait for a sign. A moment when we have gathered enough information, so we can fight."

Taytra grabs a handful of straw and throws it at the bars. "Yeah, and how are we going to fight? There are these things called bars that you already explained have magick on them. So, what is your smart plan now?"

Moraine nods. "You are right, we, as we have already said many times, are in a difficult situation. However, reacting will not help us. We must remain passive. If they trust us not to fight, we can learn things from the guards. And when we have gained enough knowledge, we can strike."

Taytra grumbles something under her breath but doesn't say anything else, just picks up a handful of hay and begins tearing it apart. "Fine, we can sit and wait. I guess."

15

Shauna

I wake up with the dawn, birds chirping merrily. As the last waves of sleep slip away, I let my thoughts drift on the melody of the bird's voices. First, they spin to the elf who lies a few feet away and to what he had said. Paulo has no one. He has every reason not to trust me, and yet without knowing me, he brought me into his sanctuary.

We are young, inexperienced and in my case at least, scared. We aren't trained to defend ourselves, but we have to protect ourselves from spellcasters who would stop at nothing to kill us.

Dark bruises are beginning to bloom on my skin where the vines had gripped my hands and legs. So maybe Paulo isn't as vulnerable as me, but the Dark Ones were still growing stronger as they slowly isolated each of the Frituals.

The night before had been a blur of action. I never had a chance to even think of the tools that Queen Moraine had given me. I reach into the depths of my bag past the food that had been hastily packed until I find a straight edge. I look over the book, it has been carefully bound in a dark midnight blue silk and a gold filament lettering that shimmers dully as I turn the book over in my hands. I dive into my bag, this time in search of the worn out dictionary. Laying the two books side by side, I open to the first page. It takes me around ten minutes to work through the complicated lettering, flipping through the yellowed pages of the dictionary looking for a simple solution to the complex words.

If you are reading this, most likely you have been dubbed the water bender of your generation. This is truly an honor. Thousands of others have been tested as they have come of age.

That is why I ask you to please heed my warning and learn from those before you. Do not cast spells that are too powerful for you. If you are tired or if you have never attempted them before the outcome could be disastrous. Even when facing the Dark Ones. There is evil in this world. An evil that will stop at nothing to harm you. For every one you kill, five more are ready to take his place. They are highly skilled spell casters and will show no mercy. They have all the black forms of magick at their beck and call. Avoid them at all costs.

Good Luck

"Who wrote this?" I ask no one in particular, closing the book to look at the cover again, I don't see an author's name inscribed on the cover. *Odd.*

"It's a conglomeration of knowledge, no specific writer," Paulo says from where he lay. "That's how my book was at least."

"Oh," I say flipping the pages. The book is nearly four hundred pages of text I will have to translate and work through before I can begin to feel like I know what I am doing.

"I wish you could have been trained by someone who knew what they were doing. But I guess I can teach you as much as I can. I am sure the exercises my teachers gave me can be adapted for water."

"Thank you, Paulo!" I say. His word of help begins to lift off the layer of pressure I felt was crushing me into the floor. "But can I ask another thing of you?" I say thinking of another flaw in my nonexistent training.

"Do I want to know that question?" he says joking.

I smile. "Well, do you know how to fight, you know with like a sword or a knife or something? Maybe in the meantime, before I can cast spells, I can fight like that."

"Seriously? Don't you know how to fight? I— ugh sorry it's just you did pretty well with that dagger."

I blush. "Yeah I am surprised I didn't drop it. I was just hoping if I hacked at the vines enough they would go away."

"Well," he says laughing, "as efficient as that method was yesterday I don't think it will work in the future. Well unless you used an ax or a morning star. But that can get, messy." My face explains clearly how little I want to do that. "Okay, that's what I thought. In the meantime would you rather learn how you use that short sword you brought or this?" He gets up and leaning against a wall where I hadn't noticed it before is a bow and a quiver full of arrows. When I nod at the bow, he places an apple in a notch in the wall and walks back to me. "Watch," he pulls an arrow from the quiver and slips it onto the string. With his arm fully extended he draws back with his other hand until the feathers of the arrow are just brushing his cheek. He looks down the shaft, aiming the shot then releases. It is a beautiful miss. The arrow flies straight to the floor below the apple, all the power gone.

Paulo laughs at his failure. "Well that's what I get for trying to show off. The steps to do it are simple, but there are a lot of factors. I would much prefer to just go at someone with a sword but, that's just me."

He pulls out another arrow like he is going to try again, but I interrupt him. "Can I try?" He looks at me for a moment like he is going to scold a student for interrupting his lesson but gives in.

He hands me the bow, and I soon see he wasn't kidding. I spend the first ten minutes trying to draw the bow back without the arrowhead falling away from the bow. Then I find I can only pull the arrow half-way, and even then the muscles in my arm are shaking.

I release the arrow feeling like it would be a good shot and no... the arrow has some power, but it is not enough to fly straight. It is enough, however, to send it flipping end over end to land next to Paulo's. "It was a nice try," he said trying to sound encouraging, but he seems to hug the wall a little more. "You will have to get some more upper body strength if you want to get a full draw. I got that bow from our armory. I think it has a sixty or seventy-pound draw."

I pull out another arrow. "I want to try a few more times."

"Are you sure? Your arms will-"

"I am sure," I say and release the arrow five feet in front of me. I do about another six shots and am no closer to my target. I can see Paulo is trying not to laugh when I plop down next to the fire and start rubbing my tense muscles. To add to the ones Paulo put there yesterday, several spots on my wrist are producing bruises. "Don't say anything, I will get this down," I say when I wince as he hands me breakfast.

"Whatever you say." He moves across the room and starts digging in one of his bags. "Next time try wearing this." He tosses a stiff leather cuff to me. I slip my hand through and tighten the strings. *It would have been helpful to have had this before letting the string lash out at my hand every time I released the string* I think.

I continue to practice until lunch, using it as a way to build strength and to focus my fears. After a lunch of cheese and fruit, I sneak out of our little camp to a stream that runs nearby to collect some water. We have plenty of water but I want something to do, I don't want to sit like a bump on a log in our little hideaway for days on end. I can feel myself starting to get antsy, but my arms are too sore from drawing back the bow to focus on that anymore.

While I was away, I did some much-needed thinking.

If there were other's, why was I chosen? Am I related? Or is as simply that the Goddess chose me? I have no answer for these questions.

Well I am told we do the tests because we need to see how you react to water. The Goddess has to be sure of her choices. Even she is not infallible a voice says seeming to brush the edge of my mind.

I immediately stiffen. *Who are you?* I ask. My mind feels full, like my thoughts have been shoved to the side to make room for another's.

You know who I am the voice says not answering the question.

I panic slightly, what if this is a Dark One? What if they got in my head? *Where did I meet you?* I focus on the dish in my hand, how smooth the canteen feels in my hand. How the water burbles around the opening send ripples as they wash away downstream.

I brought you into the council room with Moraine, we met Damian there as well. We began to discuss what happened. You looked so surprised by everything you saw. Damian snuck up on Moraine and she half scolded him.

I sighed in relief my hand straying unconsciously to where the gills had appeared on my skin. *I didn't know I could speak to you like this? Will this hurt me?*

Serena laughed lightly. *You were right to test me. No, you don't need to be afraid, all the power to do this is coming from me. You are safe. I wouldn't normally contact you like this, but I wanted you to know what was happening at home. These are different circumstances.*

16

Shauna

Alright so my family is locked up in escape proof cells, but they are unharmed right? I ask trying to process the information and not panic.

Yes they are unharmed, apart from some scratches and bruises gained fighting against their capture, no harm came to your family or the queen. I am only telling you this, so you do not go back. I can't stress this enough. If you return, you and your family will all die. You cannot be with them now.

I hang my head pushing the escape plan that had started forming in my head away. *I know, I just wish there was something I could do to help them! How did you keep from getting caught?*

I left prior to the attack. Moraine sent me to follow up on some rumors of movement. But believe me, there is something you can do, Serena said sympathetically. *Go find the others and grow strong. Then return. It is all you can do right now. When you are stronger. Then- and only then, should you come back and fight.*

"Hey, are you alright?" Paulo asks coming up behind me and scaring the living daylights out of me. "Sorry about that," he says once I have relaxed and stopped threatening him with the canteen. "You've been out here a long time. I just wanted to check on you."

I reach out to Serena but she is gone. With a sigh I turn to Paulo. "Yes I'm alright. I was just speaking with the Guardian, I met her before my ceremony. She came to me, my thoughts I mean."

"Are you sure it was her?" he asks warily.

"Positive, I made her answer some questions before I let her in completely. I'm tired now, though." I rub my head, a small throb growing. "Does talking to people like in your head drain your strength like normal magick?"

"I think so, the few times I have I have felt quite weak. Mental communicating can take a lot out of you even if another person creates the link. More than you realize you are using at that moment. Come on, we can talk more inside." He won't let me speak until I have eaten half of an apple. "Alright, we have started to get some energy back now, was it good news?"

"Sort of, has anyone spoken to you? Like recently? Since your naming ceremony, I guess," I ask putting the apple aside and wiping its sweet, sticky juices off on my skirt.

"I have, but there isn't any point. Everyone from my home that I could care about is dead."

"Oh, I am sorry I didn't mean to—"

"It's alright Shauna. I have come to terms with it," he pauses focusing on his hands. Below him, on the floor, a small flower grows, starts to wilt and die before blooming again. He is refocusing his thoughts on the new rather than the old. "It's alright, what did she say?"

"She said that they are all alive, my family and the queen," I say. "They are imprisoned in a magickally guarded cell but unhurt. She wanted me to know so I wouldn't try to go back and save them. I want to of course. But she says that the only

90

way I can protect them is to stay away," I say, a bit of bitter fear bubbling up at the end.

"Well, I guess we can be alone together right?" Paulo says with a wry smile.

* * *

The next three days I stare at the elfish text, slowly deciphering every word I can. I figure out how to make the orb again, this time, I am in control of it. I am able to make it spin high in the air and fling it around the room; I even split it into a hundred little balls. Zig-zagging through the room this way and that. Not a single droplet is out of my control. With Paulo in the center, flinching whenever one came near. But only four hit him. Okay the first time I tried it one hit him square in the face, but I was able to collect each molecule of water and try again. He said it was the weirdest feeling ever having the water there, then before it pulled free of his face.

I found another spell that allows me to extract clean, pure water from the earth. Each droplet is clean of dirt and sweet on the tongue. We will never be without water.

We both practice, learning and honing our abilities but we have limits. We don't want to become so tired we can't defend ourselves. Paulo is able to talk to the animals of the forest. They bring us roots and berries to eat. He still has to hunt for meat, though. He always looks so sad whenever he comes back. I guess he would be if he can talk to them. I would hunt for us if I knew how.

The trees multiply, and branches fall for firewood. Paulo even can enter an animal and move with them, scouting the area.

Both of us work at the bow and arrow and duel with branches Paulo has shaped into swords. I need a lighter bow. So we mainly try to spar with large branches. Clearly, this is Paulo's preferred weapon. He is skilled, and quick. If we hadn't been using sticks, I would be very dead.

"We will have to leave soon," he says after one of our sparring matches. I am doing better. By better I mean I last about two minutes. "My sparrow scouts are reporting more movement in the woods. They must sense our magick and know we are here somewhere. They still have the encampment on the plains, if we don't move soon we will be surrounded."

I am massaging my arms where he had hit a nice and painful double tap. "So what do we need to do before we move?"

"I would gather some provisions, then sleep, we'll make our move at night with the cover of darkness."

I can't help but think of the false night they had created to attack my people. Darkness makes them strong, but we can't risk being spotted in the day. "It isn't the strongest plan, I admit, but we don't have much else to go off of at the moment," he says sensing my unease at our subpar plan.

"Alright, we move at night. Let's get out of here." I walk over to the wall where the short sword I had come with lies, feeling its weight and balance. "I hope I won't have to use this." I glance up at him. "You take it."

"No, Shauna, that is a blade given to you by your Queen. I would feel wrong if I were to take it from you. I have my own tricks, don't worry about me."

I look at him half doubting him. Over the recent days we have worked so hard, but he always seems to be holding back, he has a bit more power he is storing up in case something goes wrong. I don't know enough about myself to do so. I still break out in a sweat all over my body the instant I touch any form of magick. I glow for hours, a thing Paulo says will fade faster as my body adapts to it.

I have to trust that he has the power to protect us both. "Okay let's get some sleep before we leave," I say curling up on my bedroll sensing that sleep would lay far away.

17

Shauna

"Paulo something feels wrong," I murmur as we crouch at the edge of the forest. The camps are quiet, not a single soulless Dark One in sight, not even a watchman.

"You feel it too? I thought it was just me. We have to move, though."

"Of course, we have to move. I just can't shake it." The feeling hangs in the air like the chill that comes after the rain.

I know what you mean. I say we talk like this from now on. But careful, don't say anything important they might be listening in. His voice gently settles into my head echoing slightly. After Serena spoke to me, mind communication was something we practiced. I still couldn't initiate a conversation but, I could block him, shove him out, and end a conversation, which was a good start.

I nod in approval then point to us then the plain. *Let's move. Ready?*

I'm ready. We move as quietly as we can. Crouching low in the grass trying to hide our faces in the dim light. The grass hisses as it drags across our clothes. I look under the edge of my hood and notice all the braziers. I pass my short sword between my hands wiping the clamminess off my hands on the edge of my cloak. On the ground is what seems to be a shimmering black liquid crossing the earth leading back to the braziers. *What is that?*

Paulo examines it for a moment as I keep watch. Still no movement. My heart races as anxiety flows through me. *Black magick. It's a sort of alarm, don't touch it. We don't want to alert anyone.*

Sounds good to me. We step, lightly tiptoeing, over and around the alarms. When it's gone shrinking back like snakes slithering so fast we can hardly react.

"I think my cloak hit it, it's triggered. Go run! Run!" Paulo shouts aloud forgetting about the mind link. We begin running as fast as we can, our packs thumping against our backs. "Whatever happens, run, don't look back. Don't stop!" The braziers flare flames jumping to five feet high. Dogs howl and strain at the ropes holding them still. I pull the hood of my cloak higher.

"Go Shauna go!" I push the energy from the fear I feel into my legs as men can be heard moving about.

I glance around, but I can't see Paulo. *Where did you go?* Off to my right, I hear a cord snap, and a dog is free. It is coming straight for me.

I keep running but keep it in sight. It is a huge dog. A monster of a dog. It gets closer with every step I try to get away from it. I clumsily readjust my sword. The dog jumps and I slash. In doing so I miss the dog, and I miss my step too, landing face first in the dirt. I gasp for air crawling a few feet before I push myself up.

"Shauna stop! Stop running let me help you."

Was it— no it couldn't be. I spin on my heel to face him.

"Please, Shauna let me help you," Philippe shouts running toward me.

"I— Philippe? No, I can't stop. What are you doing here? Run! Run!" I want nothing more than to stop to let myself be carried away to safety. But that wouldn't happen right now. We need to stay on the move. I can't see the dog anymore but doubt that would give up its prey, me, that easily. It is the Dark Ones. It has to be a spell. It can't be him.

"Shauna come on, let's just talk," he said before getting knocked aside by soldiers as they come running toward me.

"Philippe run!" I shriek as the Dark Ones circle me.

"Nice blade there Pretty. Wanna dance?" one sneers, he stabs at my leg, and somehow I manage to dodge it and keep moving. "You can't run forever," he says right behind me. "We have you surrounded."

I spin, sword held in front of me. It feels so heavy and useless in my hands. *It's better than nothing, right?* He is right, they are all around circling me like I am their prey.

"Back off! I'm warning you!" I say trying to sound strong, but I'm nervous, my hands are again slick with sweat and shaking from fear. I reach down and uncork the water canteen at my side. "Don't make me repeat it!"

A man jabs a sword at me, and I swing and swing trying to keep him back. Another comes from behind, and I manage to spin around just in time. My blade slices through skin and muscle as he reaches for me. The red droplets cover me as he screams in pain holding the arm to his chest. I splutter at the metallic taste coating my lips and try to smear it away before another man takes his place as he falls back. I try to run through the gap that opens but they push me back, and they creep inward, their swords a ring of death around me.

"Get away from me!" I screech as they swarm me. "Barak aka tura!" I shout, and the soldiers finally take a step back. Water flows from the canteen on my hip and slips into my hand. It slides down like a snake coiling in my hand, floating above the ground. I look around trying to intimidate them and snap my water whip once, twice. They try to slash at it, but it does nothing for them. The whip is water, but when I strike at them, it is like supple leather. But if they try they pass straight through it and then it reforms. They lunge again, and I snap the whip. It leaves a large red welt across one man's face, inches from his eyes. I reach to the ground where my sword has fallen and hold it in my other hand, ready to strike. I grip the blade hard hoping that if I put all of my attention into the way my fingers gripped the hilt, they won't see my hands shake.

"Shauna, it doesn't have to be this way," Philippe says pushing his way into the circle.

"Philippe, what the Hell are you doing? Run, get away from them!"

"Shauna, you don't have to fight anymore. You are safe here."

"Safe? Are you kidding me?" I spin away from him keeping the Dark Ones always in my sight. "What did they do to you?"

"They didn't do anything to me," he says placing a hand on my shoulder.

"Get away from me!" I growl raising the whip, locking eyes with him.

"You won't hurt me," he says so arrogantly.

"And what makes you so sure of that?" I ask even though I know that he is right. I won't hurt him, not bad at least. My arm still has blisters from him. "Look what they did to our home? They locked everyone up!"

"Let's stop this now and talk." He makes a motion like wiping away dirt from a window and with a hiss my whip is gone vaporized into nothing.

"I— how did you do that?" I ask stunned. I think about calling more water to me, but I can already feel the draining effects of the whip.

"Those answers will come in time, just go with me now," he says pulling me to him, and he even goes as far as to pull the sword from my hand.

Shauna are you alright, I—

No not now, go, I say shoving against him, pushing him out of my mind.

But— Paulo says pushing back against me, trying to stay.

Get away Paulo! I say pushing him away mentally as I struggle physically to get away from Philippe.

"Stop fighting Shauna, you are safe now," Philippe says pinning my hands behind me and wrapping a cord around them. "Stop fighting please, if he sees you fighting it won't work. They will hurt you. Stop. We can be together this way."

"What are you talking about? Please just let me go! If I were truly safe, you wouldn't tie me up!" I strain against the cords binding me. They cut deep into my skin but hold. "Why? Why are you with them? Why are you tying me up? Just let me go!"

"I can't do that- you must know I can't," he says shaking his head.

I manage to pull myself away from him and stumble. The drained feeling that comes from using my powers is settling over my body. I will have to use the remaining strength I have to get myself free, even if it could be dangerous. "Aka huden das— mehheh." Philippe cuts me off covering my mouth.

"NO! No more spells! He will hurt you!"

"Who? Philippe, you are making no sense? He will hurt me if I fight? What are you talking about?" I snap when he moves his hand away.

"He is talking about me," a voice says from behind Philippe, who gives me a pained look then releases me and turns.

"How— But you—you died! I watched my sister kill you!"

Damian just grins. "Oh don't worry, I did die. However, my friends here know dark magick, obviously. A little ritual or two and here I am." He pulls up the front of his shirt "I still have this. I think I will return the favor to your sister."

My face grows very hot, and I have to bite my tongue not to scream a slew of obscenities at him.

He just laughs at me. "Oh don't hold back, and I want to hear what you have to say," he says bending to pluck up my fallen blade. A fat lot of good that it did me. "Why don't you tell me where your friend is?"

"I don't know what you are talking about," I say eyeing the blade still speckled with the soldier's blood.

He touches the point of the sword to my shoulder putting a little pressure on it. "I think you do," Damian says and pulls the point along the edge of my dress.

"I don't know."

He presses harder, stopping the point in the hollow of my throat. "I don't just think you do, I know you do. You are with the earth Fritual. My brethren have been looking for him for a long time. Where is he?"

"I don't." He presses the blade in, and I try not to wince as I feel it pierce my skin. Hot sticky blood slips down my chest. I swallow. "I don't know where he is," I croak. Damian looks at me disbelieving every word. "We didn't tell each other where we would go. We didn't want to both get caught by you."

He pulls the blade back and stabs it into the ground. "You told me she would cooperate," He snaps at Philippe.

"I thought she would! She-"

"Shut up, stop your stammering."

"Did you really think I would be willing to go with you?" I say, wishing yet again I was free so that I could fight. To show what I had taught myself.

"Get her in a tent," Damian says with a wave of his hand.

18

Paulo

Paulo runs low to the ground. He has his sword out ready to strike. *Where should I go? Where can I meet Shauna? I need a place where we can both hide.* He looks around, not a single guard or soldier is after him. But Shauna is no longer by his side. Has he gone too fast? He calls to her with his thoughts as he peers into the darkness, still moving away from the camp and the blazing braziers. *Shauna are you alright?*

No not now go, she shouts, shutting down the link between them.

But? He tries to keep the link just long enough.

Get away Paulo. Then she is gone.

Damn it, He thinks to himself, he was stupid. The plan had fallen through. Plan? It hadn't even been close to a feasible plan.

He doesn't know what had happened. They had split apart, but he thought she was close to him, maybe twenty feet away but then the noises were farther off, and he could only see a group of soldiers. He knew he had to help, but he couldn't give himself away. That was what they had decided.

"If anything happens, we run. We leave the other," Shauna

had said. "We need to stay safe. Even if that only means one of us." They had decided that if one escaped and was able to gain the upper hand, they could come back. "Like my family. Leave me, or I will leave you and come back when either one of us has the upper hand. They can't have both of us."

He keeps moving forward, keeping his eyes and ears peeled for any sound that could be the enemy coming after.

He stops moving when he hears someone say "Hello?" It was a girl's voice.

That isn't Shauna, he thinks to himself crouching low in the grass.

"What is going on over there? Who did they kidnap?" The voice just keeps talking. "Oh, she is furious, she is fighting them! Yes, go! Oh, her sword it's gone. It's oh wait, no, he stopped."

Paulo tries not to listen, but he cant help it, he need to know what happened to her. *Shauna, we were safe. We should have just stayed in the forest.* But even as he thinks it he knows it is futile. If they had stayed much longer they both would have been taken.

"Oh, her face! She is just like me. She is a Fritual," the voice says in a softer tone.

"Wait what!?" Paulo says out loud "Who are you? Where are you?" Moving to where he could have sworn the voice had come from, the grass stands tall, unmarked by movement through the grass. "Hello?" He asks quietly, slipping his knife half out of his belt. He doesn't dare use magick now.

"I am right here," the voice says from the air. Paulo looks up. A girl with a mane of frizzy hair and soft face is floating thirty feet in the air above Paulo's head.

"I— Uh how did you? How?"

A soft breeze blew across the grass and then the girl is sitting there next to him. "Hello, I am Lyra, can you guess who I am?" she says with a smile seeing the other elf's shocked face. "Well come on, I know you can talk."

"Oh sorry, I, it's just what are doing here? Shouldn't you be like a hundred fifty miles away from here right now?" He blinks against the soft yellow glow that emanates from her trying to see her facial features in the dark. She said she was like Shauna.

"I will explain that in a bit once we get to a safer place, but what is your name?" she asked beginning to crawl away.

"Oh, right, Paulo. My name is Paulo. What about Shauna?" he stammers, hurrying after her.

"Come on, I know a place where we can hide for a bit. Your friend is under lock and key now. Those Dark Ones have been waiting for almost a week for her," she calls over her shoulder.

"Yeah, I know," he said thinking back to the safe little tree house they had back in that forest. *Shauna?* He tries. *Shauna? I don't know if you can hear me, but we are getting there, only two more.*

19

Jamie

"I want Jamie Flynn," a guard says after stomping the butt of his spear firmly on the ground. "Flynn," He repeats poking him in between the bars with the butt of his spear. "Come on, get up."

"Who's asking?" Jamie mumbles sleepily, rolling to his feet.

"The man in charge upstairs. Come on, get moving."

"You can't take him. I won't let you," Taytra says jumping to block her father's path. "Wait, you? You're Richard Henderson! Why are you with them? You are one of us!" she asks, recognition and betrayal flashing across her face.

"I used to be Richard. I have to become one of them. Every family had to give them someone as collateral. To keep the others safe and to stop rebellions," he explains as he carefully examines the floor, all the soldier-like bravado was gone.

"It that why you are taking away my father?"

He shakes his head. "No, look, I have already said too much, but your family and Philippe's are different. They won't hurt you, they want you safe and close so they can use you. That's why you are down here. Now we need to go, they will be waiting."

Jamie nods and gives Taytra a squeeze. "I'll be back before you know it."

Moraine puts a hand on Taytra's shoulder as they two watch the men walk down the hall.

"You can't act like you know me up there, we both could be in danger if we do," Richard says, fear masked by a fake power he had been given.

Jamie nods, he can't help but wonder what they wanted with him. He and Taytra are normal, nothing special or magickal about them.

Where was Shauna? Was she still safe? Was she still alive?

The double doors open, and Richard pushes Jamie inside. Men in all black stand in rows before a cool black throne, that has an almost incandescent shimmer, like grease. Moraine's throne is knocked off to the side; a rich dark burn defaces the center of the back. Jamie makes a note not to tell Moraine that they had destroyed it. This new throne is a mockery of the Queen's. "Jamie Flynn."

"Uh yes, that's me," Jamie replies a little unsure of what he should do. Who is this elf?

"I am Lord Nurzan, high commander of all the Dark Ones. All men answer to me. Those among my men and those under them."

"Well, I don't know why you would want to talk to me, sir I am the lowest of the low. I am not with you, I am the father of your enemy. Surely I can be of no good use to you," Jamie says, hoping this is a good train of thought. One that won't get him killed.

"You would think that, but that reason makes you extremely useful to me."

"Useful?" Jamie asks, his voice cracking slightly as the dark man stands and stalks towards him.

Richard shoves Jamie to his knees causing Jamie to wince, clutching his hands into fists so he wouldn't show his emotions to this elf. "Exactly human, useful. Your daughter is one of the last Frituals to reveal themselves. Now, she has found others, and I need to know where they are."

"But I don't know where they are?"

"No, but she does."

20

Shauna

Philippe stands by and watches as I fight against the guards that force me through the camp. They parade me like a cow for judging, some calling out jeers. One Dark One, an elf who must have stood a foot taller than me walks up and stops our procession. He just stares at me, pinning me down with his eyes, I flinch when he touches me. A single fingertip sliding along my jaw and down my neck before Damian gets tired and barks an order for him to stand down.

I am brought to a large tent in the middle of the camp. They throw me into a sturdy wooden chair and begin to tie me down. I do manage to kick one of the guards in the mouth before he pulls the rope taught. He spits the blood and a tooth in my face before completing the job and making sure that the knot is uncomfortably tight around my ankle.

"I wish you would listen," Philippe whispers in my ear. Trying to brush a strand of hair from my face.

I turn my face away. "Right, and where would that have gotten me? In the same exact place," I snap pulling against the ties around my limbs.

"She's right of course," Damian says pushing his way into

the tent.

"But you, you promised. You told me you wouldn't hurt her," he says like a petulant child.

This sniveling man before me is not the man I agreed to marry. But I want— need him to come back.

"I lied," Damian says simply. With a flick of his wrist thin black bands wrap around my throat ready to tighten in an instant. I freeze, feeling the oily coil slithering about my neck. They look just like the cords that had signaled the alarms that led to this situation.

"Why would you believe him? You're so stupid!"

"Again she is right; you are quite dull. You are useful to me- but not the smartest." The cord around my neck tightens slightly making it a bit harder to breathe. The end grows until it stretches from my neck to Damian's hand like I am on a leash. He gives it a jerk, testing its strength. "Get out," he says to Philippe. "Shauna and I need some time to get to know each other."

Philippe halts at the door like he is unsure what to do. My Philippe, the hothead who doesn't care what anyone thought of our relationship, would have decked this elf. When Phillippe just stands staring at me, Damian calls a few of his honchos to take him away. Their contact is what he needs, and he snaps out of it and begins fighting to get back at my side.

I can hear Philippe continuing to call to me for a few minutes after he was sent away. *Why does he keep yelling?* I wonder. *He is just going to get himself hurt.*

I take this moment of silence to assess my situation. I am tied up to a chair. My bag is gone, luckily we had thought to give all the books to Paulo so he could take the extra weight. My arms are going numb from the tight ropes holding my arms out. *I am alone, Paulo is free, at least as far as I know and I have no way to find out.*

"What are we thinking about in here?" Damian asks leaning over and tapping my temple. I decide it is best not to answer him. "Stubbornness will not help you; it will get you hurt."

I look away, looking anywhere but at him. I follow the line of the pole up to the center of the tent where the fabric is held up. Following one of the folds of fabric down my eyes stop on a large map.

The map is a detailed topography of the world. It shows all the mountains and valleys and lakes. All across the surface charcoal has been smudged to mark the rising power and control. I stare carefully at the detailed memorizing as much as I can.

"Alright, that's enough daydreaming. It is time for the two of us to talk. To get to know each other."

Damian stands and waves his hand in a circle, muttering something under his breath. It starts as a tiny pinprick of darkness, but under his caresses, it grows sucking all the light from the tent.

"Now let's begin our little interview, here's an easy one. What is your name?"

"Shauna Flynn." I see no harm in telling him something he already knows.

"What are you?"

"Aka—"

"In the common tongue." A black band weaves itself around my wrist, too tight for comfort.

"The water Fritual," I say quickly, confused by the need for common tongue and the anger that flashes in his eyes.

"Who is your family?" he asks toying with another black band.

109

"You already know the answer to that question," I say stiffly.

He smiles, but there is no joy in it. "You're right I do. But I want you to tell me. Remember? We are friends."

I have to hold back a laugh. We are anything but friends "Why should I trust you?"

The black band in his hand changes, melting into an inky black blade. "Technically speaking you shouldn't trust me. However, I feel like given the circumstances you will answer my questions."

"And if I don't?" I probe, trying to see just how far he is willing to go. He is ready to hurt me I am sure, but I also know he needs me.

"If you won't answer me. Then well I guess we will have to ask your father what to do."

"What?" I say, pulling at the ties in an attempt to get closer. The black disk begins shimmering. The ripples are changing, coalescing until it starts to create the picture of my father. "Father? How— I?"

"Shauna— Shauna are you okay? Tell me you're alright," he says cutting me off.

An unseen hand comes out of nowhere cuffing Father. "Shut it."

"Hey! Do you have to do that?" I say ignoring the feeling of the blade pressing into my throat.

"Now will you answer my questions?" Damian asks pressing the blade into my throat a touch more.

"Do I have to answer that question? I mean clearly, you know who they are I shouldn't have to tell you," I snap glancing at my father inside the dark disk.

"Fine, we will simply move on to the next question. Queen Moraine performed the final ceremony to mark the beginning of your training. In doing so, she gave you these markings correct?"

"Well I guess, you saw me then, and I didn't have them, and now I do, so what do you think? You don't know how to do a good investigation do you?"

A flash of anger goes across Damian's face then the blade at my neck presses deeper into my throat. I feel the first drop of blood slide down my neck. "You will tell me how she did it, now!" he orders.

Telling the truth would be a lot easier, however, how much damage will the answer bring me in the end? "I don't know," I say. Someone takes a blade out and places it against my father's temple. Jamie winces but makes no sound as his captors drag the blade down the side of his face. "Look stop; please stop! Why did you have to bring him into this? You didn't even give me a chance before you began threatening me." I watch the blood pool in the cut and run down the side of his face.

"Would you have answered my questions if I had not threatened your father?"

"Look, I will speak to you if I know he is not harmed alright?" I snap.

"Then answer my questions." He throws a pointed look at the image and the blade sliding down Jamie's face moves away but hovers over his skin. The tip had been close, only an inch away from the artery in his neck.

Damian gives me a look, and before the blade could creep back to his skin again, I blurt out, "Yes she did the ceremony. She spoke these words in elven. I don't know what she said it – it sounded like an ancient dialect. I couldn't make out what she was saying." It's a lie of course, but I have to use something.

Damian isn't buying it. "You mean with all those classes

you have taken, and all those books you have read you couldn't translate a single measly word for me?" he asks his voice almost sing-song as he takes a finger and traces the delicate tattoo on my face. "Come now; I know you are smarter than that."

"Well I knew what Aka and Fritual meant obviously, and a lot sounded familiar, but I couldn't quite get it. Not that fast, I was never very good at translations."

He sneers dropping his hand away from me in disgust. He looks from me to the image of my father, and with a wave of his hand, he is gone. The next instant he is on me, his hand in my hair pulling my head painfully to the side. "Do you honestly expect me to believe that?"

"Well yes," I wince as his grip grows tighter. "It is the truth." His lips press together in a narrow line, again I wonder how much he is willing to hurt me. He has to be working for someone, but would that person care if I had been hurt? My instincts tell me no. He holds my gaze for another moment before swiping a blade from a table and sticking it straight into my arm. "What— why?" I splutter in pain as blood runs down my wrist, pooling in my palm.

"This blade is a truth blade. After I make the first cut it will cut you again every time you lie." The happy glint that gives me the chills is back.

"A truth blade?"

"Did I stutter?" Anger making those terrifying eyes seem to burn.

"No, I – I just." Pain clutters my words.

He grins, "Let's begin, did you understand what Moraine had said in the ceremony?"

I watch the blade weighing out my options. "Yes I understood what she said to me. But I can't repeat enough for it to be helpful."

"We will see about that," he almost purrs. "Next question, where is your friend the Earth Fritual?"

"I don't know," Damian stares hard at the blade hovering above my skin. But it does not move.

21

Paulo

P aulo can't sleep, not when he doesn't know what is happening to Shauna. He can't try to contact her - not with the Dark Ones listening in. Paulo had tried briefly, but she had put up a wall that was too thick for him to get through. He rolls over again onto his back. Lyra had brought him to a cave she had found on the mountain just across the plain. The roof of the cave arches above him about ten feet. There is a small hole in the ceiling like a rabbit had tried to build a den but too late realized its mistake. It did make a good smoke hole for the tiny fire in the center of the cave.

Lyra lies fast asleep a few feet away; her face is calm and serene. It is like she is able to take all the worries of the day and cast them aside like water rolling over a waterfall. This girl he had just met is the next step in his journey, and he knows nothing about her. *Was this how Shauna had felt meeting me? How long did it take for her to really trust me? No,* he thinks. *I can't think like that, they would want that. But I— I can just peek, right?* Slowly he rises to a low crouch and begins to move to Lyra's small bag. He lifts open the leather pouch. Inside there is a small bundle of herbs wrapped in a large leaf, a roll of bandages, some berries and fruits and a small bag of coins. Paulo sits back on his heels. He has learned nothing except that Lyra packed only the necessities and kept it small.

"I have to pack light; it's easier for me to travel flying the way I do if I pack light," the elf says sitting up.

"I—I," Paulo stammers, his ears flushing bright red, he searches for something to say, a way to excuse himself but he has been caught. He still has her bag open in his hand. "I'm sorry," he finally mumbles quickly putting the bag back in its original location.

"It's quite alright; you are trying to figure out what kind of person I am. I did the same thing when you dozed off for a bit earlier," she replies simply. "How do you travel carrying all that gear, all those books?"

Paulo looks at the large pile of books, food, and weapons he has been carrying. "Part of it is Shauna's, she thought it would be better if I carried the more valuable items, so we could get away faster, I'm a better fighter than her," he trailed off.

Lyra comes and sat next to him. "So, what?" she asks with large eyes full of sympathy.

He stares hard at his hands. "So, I am a better fighter. I was supposed to protect her, and I didn't. I didn't even know she was in trouble until it was too late. I was going to protect her. I was going to protect her, so I wouldn't lose her too, like my brother. They killed him to get to me and now I'm going to lose my only friend left."

"Hey," Lyra puts a hand on his arm. "We will get her back. We will make a plan and get her back; then you will have two friends." Paulo looks up at her, a small light back in his eye. "Don't worry; I have a plan. Go to sleep now; we will start in the morning," Lyra said lying back down.

Paulo wants to ask for more information. That small bite of hope doesn't feel like enough. "Get some sleep; I will keep watch. Being dead on your feet won't help your friend."

22

Barin

Flames dance along the walls flickering over his black uniform. How long had he been standing here now? Seven, eight hours? Looking over at nothing. A single soul is up on the wall with Barin, another guard; he doesn't know who he is. Must've been from another division. Barin scans the horizon again, but the only thing that moves is the leaves on the trees in the distance. With the hand not holding his staff, he begins pinching and releasing the skin on his thigh. The pressure on his skin burns but it brings a bit of clarity to his mind.

"Our watch should be over soon," the other guard says, he gestures casually in the direction the sun will rise. "You can make out the dawn." Barin looks where the man is pointing with skepticism. There is a faint glow on the horizon, but that isn't the sun. They are guarding the wall on the western front. If the sun is rising from there, they have bigger problems. There was a city that way. A once great city that Barin had lived in for most of his life. It had at one point been a magnificent city, but the Dark Ones had captured it for themselves. But that glow is from hundreds of torches and fires of those without homes.

"I am sorry to disappoint you friend, but that is not the sun. That was the city of Bulandon. The lights you see are all the bonfires the people must light now to keep warm now that the city has been razed and all their homes destroyed," he says bitterness creeping into his voice.

"Oh. You sound like you have some opinions on that, one that shouldn't be shared while we're in this uniform."

Barin looks out at his lost Bulandon. "It happened a long time ago."

Barin hears the scrape of boots on the stone stairs and turns to see his father coming up the steps with two guards. An escort or their replacement? "How is the watch Barin? Anyone from Bulandon come and bother us again?"

"No sir," Barin replies. He thinks of the woman and two children who had come recently, begging for help. She was gaunt and filthy; she had been giving all her food to her children. She asked for help, and they had refused her help because of her children's imperfect skin. They had called them half-breeds, things less than nothing, that the children were disgusting. Barin thought that the people he served were the disgusting ones. She fought screaming that it wasn't fair, that her choice to marry a human shouldn't harm her children. She was taken away, and the doctor came back shortly saying the mother had died of exhaustion. Barin almost believed that diagnosis. He never heard what happened to the children. He didn't think he wanted to know either.

"No signs of movement here or there coming from Bulandon."

"Excellent, you two are relieved of your duties for the night, but Barin, I would like to see you in my chambers, I will have a breakfast laid out for you after you change," his father says.

Barin notices there is no room to alter the request. His father did that, laying out a step by step order with no way to deviate from it.

"I will be there shortly," Barin says imagining the hot bath he could have taken to leech the cold night from his skin.

"Good, I will expect you in my chambers in no more than thirty minutes." He turns and goes back down the ramparts, his officer's cape billowing behind him.

"Your father is the General Nurzan?" the guard who Barin had been with all night asks in disbelief.

"Yes, the General Nurzan is my father. No, I won't report you for anything you said or did tonight. I am not a spy. I am a fellow soldier like you," Barin says in a dry, monotone voice.

"I'm guessing you get that a lot. I'm sorry, you seem a lot more relaxed than him."

"That is because I am not him. I am his son, but we are not the same elf." Barin hated when people compared him to his father. When people put it together, when they stood next to each other and people realized that they had the same dark tone to their skin, that they had the same eye color, and posture which Barin hated more than anything. 'You guard just like your father used to. We know you will make it far within our ranks.' He hated it. "People forget that we are not just like our fathers, we have mothers too."

The other elf nods in agreement. "So what is your mother like?"

Barin's chest tightens, he hadn't meant to mention mothers, his mother. "She is dead. We killed her."

"What? You killed your mother?"

"No, no, not me," Barin says quickly. "This order did. The Dark Ones. She didn't believe in the same things my father did. She told him what he was doing was wrong." Barin pauses. "She told him she was going to help the people in Bulandon, his reply was if she went he couldn't stop the soldiers from attacking her. She went anyway."

The guard is quiet. "Oh, I'm sorry, I never thought Lord Nurzan would have a wife who was a-"

"Don't!" Barin snaps. "Don't you dare call her that. My mother was not a radical. She just wanted peace and the Dark Ones don't." He turns and stalks to his room. He shuts the door and leans on it, taking deep breaths and pushing away the emotions that come with talking about his broken family. Barin hated his father and all that he did. All he did and thought about was destroying things. His mother had been a creatress. She knew some of the old magick; she used to play with him, blowing him around with wind, picking him up. He had never been happier than when he was playing with his mother.

He begins changing his clothes, peeling the cold ones off his body and throwing them over by the fire. Barin moves over to the fire, standing close to its heat. He can feel it almost burning his skin; it feels tight and hot, painful after the cold night. He stands there a few more seconds before moving to his trunk, pulls out a few more articles of black clothing and looks identical to how he had ten minutes ago on the ramparts.

He grabs his sword, his father had given it to him, buckles it around his waist and makes his way from his room to his father's on the floor above. He wonders what his father had found to lecture him about this time. Last he had heard his father had been called to Cabineral, *What would bring him back so quickly?* He must have taken on of his stronger attendants if he was able to make the jump to Cabineral and back in a under a week.

Something must have happened. And now he was going to get a lecture on loyalty. Barin was never a good enough Dark One. He was too much like his mother, said as an insult, but he wanted to be like his beautiful mother, so it doesn't sting like the others. He wonders if anyone had reported him talking about his mother, but that had been after he had been summoned. He climbs the stairs that had once led to a king's chambers; his father loved to gloat on the fact. "I live in the palace of a king," he would say. "I sleep in his room, I write at his desk. Does this make me a king?"

Barin knocks on the door three times. "Enter," his father calls. Upon entering, Barin is surprised by just how many scrolls are all over the room. General Nurzan never was messy, he needed organization everywhere to function, but now he is harried, his eyes jump from page to page reading and recording things in a small black notebook. "Ah, Barin, perfect. Sit." His voice is as calm and silky as ever. "Now, this disaster might surprise you."

"Just a little."

The general keeps talking like he hasn't heard Barin at all, "but there is a reason for it. You know that old monk we captured when we took Bulandon, he thinks that now the Spirit Fritual will surface. Finally, I have been searching for years."

Barin rolls his eyes, then quickly looks down hoping his father won't notice. The Dark Ones had taken Bulandon on a rumor that the Spirit Fritual was there already, though the test hadn't been done in years. Every so often another rumor would surface, but nothing came of it. "What makes him so sure now?"

"Water and fire were found Barin. We have now seen all but Spirit."

Barin grips the arms of the chair. "What? Both how?"

"They came from the same city, they both were from Cabin-eral. Fire hasn't been tested yet, Damian's men caught the Fire Fritual on the way to Fueguasta peak; I have reports of all four fire, water, earth, and wind being in the same area. But I'm not sure if they are together. Spirit must surface now and be with them. I will catch them."

Barin liked to sit and talk with the old monk, Alois, sometimes when he wasn't on duty. The old elf was very knowledgeable and didn't judge him for his patronage. He had known the boy's mother. "So, what will you do?"

For the first time since Barin walked in Nurzan looks up. "I am not going to do anything, you are." Barin is confused. "You are going back to Bulandon and will talk to the people, you will find him."

"You want me to be the one to hunt for him or her this time?" Barin doesn't like this. His father is using Barin's want to go home, in conjunction with his needs.

"Of course, you will be more useful to me doing this than sitting up on a wall for eight hours at a time. You will go on a sort of undercover mission to Bulandon and stay there for a time. I have already bought and had a room furnished for you. You simply need to get on a horse and go."

"Father," Barin pauses searching for words. "You know it is my deepest wish to go home, but there are quite a few things I still don't understand. How will I even know when I find the Fritual? There isn't some sign that says this is me. They haven't been tested, they won't have markings to distinguish them from the average person. I won't know if they are human or elf. As that seems to be an option now. It makes the search even harder."

Nurzan laughs. "Do you think I would send my only son out

there blind? This book has all the notes that I think that you will need. But, I know our fighting styles vary, and you will want to attack this mission from a different angle. So..." He opens a drawer and pulls out a large silver key. "Take the key, and this book and go and speak with the monk. Do whatever you need to do to get the information you need." He hands the two items to Barin. "You had best not fail me in this. I need to find this Fritual."

"Yes Father, I will do as you wish. When must I leave?"

"I told the guard tower that you will have work for the next few weeks that will take you away from here starting in this afternoon. So, go and rest, you can begin after you have slept."

23

Barin

After his meeting, Barin returns to his room where he sleeps for a few hours before waking up feeling clammy and tense. His dreams had been flashbacks of his mother dragging him out of bed and through the burning city of Bulandon before it had fallen. His father hadn't warned his mother when they were going to attack. He remembers the buildings crumbling around him and the magick. He knows what it was now but then, when he had first seen it, it had terrified him. He still feels the hair on the back of his neck rises whenever he sees the black coils.

He goes to the water pitcher and splashes cool water on his face and neck, trying to wash away the memories that he knows are going to haunt him for the next few weeks as he stays in Bulandon. He grabs a towel off the stand and begins patting his face dry. He looks up into the mirror and notices for the first time how tired he looks. Being on for the night duties is hard. His days are flipped. He can't remember the last time he woke with the sunrise.

He sits on the bed and grabs the notebook his father has given him. The notes inside had started out as neat little notes in bullet point lists. Barin can see where his father has gotten excited by the things he was finding, drawing arrows and inserting page references. Just decoding this notebook will take weeks, following every piece of his father's mind as it went along. This mind map is how his father's mind worked. Barin sighs and snaps the book shut.

He opens the wardrobe and pulls out the few articles of clothing that he owns that aren't black and pulls them on. A pair of dark brown trousers and a green shirt. He pulls on his boots, the same pair he has owned for several years that he just keeps getting re-soled. He doesn't make enough money being a guard to buy a new pair. He shoves a few more possessions in a bag: The notebook, a pencil, an extra shirt and pants, and some socks. He reaches up to the top of his wardrobe and pulls down his sword and a small knife, sliding it into his boot. He slings the bag over his shoulder and as he looks around the room, buckles on the sword. There isn't much in the room itself beside these belongings. He is about to leave when he turns back and lifts his mattress pulling out a small picture frame. It is a sketch of his mother. Barin knows he isn't what she would have wanted him to be, he isn't what he wanted to be. If Barin is honest with himself, he doesn't know what he wants to be. He opens his bag back up and gingerly places the photo of his mother in the bag wrapped up in a shirt to keep it safe. Barin scans the room one more time. Sure he will be back here soon, but for now, he feels a sense of dread stepping out of the door.

Barin walks through the halls and for not the first time he realizes how trapped he has always felt there. The walls feel constricting. There isn't a single window. The only time he sees the outside world is spent sitting on top of a wall looking out into the black of night. He feels the weight of his father's position crushing him. The eyes that follow him expecting him to be just like him. If he makes a move out of line he was a "radical" like his mother. He likes going and talking to "the monk" as his father calls him. Barin smiles; if his father knew just how well he already knew Alois, he would be rather annoyed. Barin runs up the stairs to the tower three at a time. He could make it in eight strides. He counted every time he went up to meet with the elf. He knocks four times. His little code with Alois that it was him and not some other guard coming to be cruel to him. "Alois, I am coming in," he says in the tough voice guards used so that if anyone were listening, they would think that he was doing a routine check in on the elf.

"Enter at your own will," the elf replies.

Barin opens the door to find Alois sitting at the crude box he uses as a writing desk. He had been giving an old food crate to "Do whatever is monks do." He has worn the surface down from use so much that the sides are a much darker color than the top. It is splattered with bits of wax from the many candles Barin had brought the elf that he has burned through in his time in the cell. He took rocks and made them into legs so that the "desk" would sit on Alois' lap and be propped up a bit closer to him.

"Master Barin, to what do I owe the pleasure of this visit?" Alois asks beginning to slide out from under his desk.

"Please, don't get up friend," Barin motions coming down to sit next to his friend. "This visit is not of my own will. Though you know, I love to come and visit you. I am sorry that I haven't come to visit you recently."

Alois shrugs. "It is alright Barin, your father has had me busy working on this absurd list of traits of a Fritual for him."

"So, you already know why I am here then," Barin sighs leaning against the wall. "I thought that it was pointless."

"You are much wiser than your father on that front. There is a reason that we do the tests. Or did. We don't know who the Fritual is. There normally aren't traits that are made apparent until they have been tested. From what I can gather from the reports your father has given me, the fire Fritual was a different case. But I believe that that was caused by the stress and fear of losing his loved one. Perhaps being around others who were casting magick triggered it, I don't think his powers would have been revealed in any other way."

Barin pulls out the notebook that his father had given him. "He gave me this, I can't really piece together what he means. Though I only glanced at it before I came up here."

Alois flips through the pages, turning back and forth between notes Nurzan had created. "I follow the train of thought, but just. He clearly spent a lot of time searching for this person. Which we already knew. I do not mean to offend, but your father is obsessed with finding the Frituals."

Barin nods. "The spirit Fritual in particular. He won't admit it, but he is guilty. He destroyed his home to find a person based on a rumor. My mother died because of that rumor. I think he feels like if he finds them, it might validate some of all that happened. I don't believe it will though."

Alois sighs. "Those rumors circle every year. Your father was just overtaken by the idea of the Dark Ones at the time to believe what anyone would tell him. How long have they had their control over him?"

"Well, Bulandon fell four years ago now. So about five years?" Barin pauses. "Alois? How come none of the other kingdoms came to help us?"

The elf sighs. "That is something I myself would very much like to know. One of the reports I was able to get smuggled in here said that the Elven kingdoms had stopped communicating, so they thought we had exiled them. It makes sense for the elves. I question how the world of men didn't hear. Their timelines are much shorter than ours. That should be something you try to understand when you leave. I would love to know." Alois pulls a pencil out of his pocket and opens to the next blank page in the notebook. "I knew some men in Bulandon that might be willing to give you some information about what has happened in the time since the fall. I wouldn't say who you are, but say that you know me."

Barin looks at the note. It reads Janson Scott 57 River Lane. "What am I looking for?"

"I don't know if it is still there," Alois replies scooting out from under his desk and plucking up another candle as the one on his desk begins to sputter out. "But it was once a tavern, Janson was the owner." He lights the wick of the new candle then holds the base of the candle over the still burning candle to melt the base before sticking it down on his desk.

"Alright, um Alois do you have any idea where I should look for him if he isn't there anymore? Like a house? Wait, this sounds familiar." He dug through his bag for the notebook "Yes, this is where my father has bought a room. Does Mr. Jansen live elsewhere? Do you think this tavern was taken over?"

The elf shakes his head. "No, the Tavern was his home. He named it after his horse The Pretty Penny. I didn't think she was a pretty penny. That was the most stubborn horse I had ever met. If it still goes by the same name his is the one running it."

Barin laughs. "Alright."

"Thank you. I hope Janson and his family are alright, it has been years." Barin thinks of when the Dark Ones had brought the monk in. They had kept him in the dungeons far below. But Nurzan grew tired of having to walk all the way to the dungeon whenever he wanted to question the elf, so he ordered him to be moved to the tower cell, whose staircase was just down the hall from Nurzan's room.

"So, what is on this list my father has commissioned you to create for me?' Barin asks plucking the page from the desk. "Facial markings, I thought those wouldn't show until after the ceremony that you would have to perform."

"You and I know this. Your father might not." Alois says with a shrug.

"The ability to control others' emotions, reading another's thoughts. Perhaps moving things by thought. You don't really know what I need to look for do you?"

Alois shakes his head. "Most of the records that we had for those that could control some aspects of the spirit magick were destroyed when the Dark Ones sacked the city. It isn't our fault. I have requested all that I can, but your father refuses to let me go into the city to try to find anything. And since they have been slowly killing of the royalty not many who are able to control it still live."

Barin looks at his old friend, who has so much knowledge. "Perhaps now he will let you if I go with you to 'watch over you'. I could really use the company," Barin says.

Alois' eyes sparkle. "You have no idea how much I would give to get out of this cell and be able to walk in the light of day." He slumps slightly. "I doubt your father would allow it."

Barin grins. "He told me I had any tools I needed at my disposal. You are a tool that I need and want by my side of course."

"Well then, what are you waiting for? Go and talk to your father." Alois grins. "It isn't like I will be going anywhere while I wait for you."

Barin rushes down the stairs and quickly feels the sense of optimism fade as he steps down the stairs. How could he convince his father that he needed Alois, without letting on to the fact that he knew more about him then he had initially let on?

He stops at the door and listens for a moment to see whether or not his father is in a meeting with some of his generals. If he is, Barin will have to wait until it is over. There was no way that he was going to get what he needed if the other officers were there. His father was all show when he wasn't alone. Barin presses his ear up to the door and hears the pop and crackle of the fire. But no other voices.

Barin lifts his hand to knock when his father comes around the corner. "Ah, Barin ready to go off into the city?"

"Hello Father, that is actually what I came to talk to you about."

Nurzan pulls a key out of his pocket and unlocks the door to his room. "Yes, of course, what can I help you with? Do you need some of my reports?"

"I took your advice. I looked through the notes that you gave me then I went and spoke with Alo— the monk. He had such a great wealth of knowledge that there was no way I would be able to get it all down. He suggested places to go visit — if they are still there and people to go find that might know things. He will be a great asset to me. However, I feel like that if I leave now I won't be fully equipped with the amount of knowledge I would need to properly execute your mission. I feel like I would benefit more if he were with me."

Nurzan's eyes narrow. "Did the monk suggest this to you?"

"No Father," Barin says quickly "I suggested this of my own accord. He would stay in the apartments that you have procured for me unless I needed his help to find a place or a person that he suggested that I visit. He simply would be there as a guide for me to bounce ideas and information that I have procured off of."

Barin mentally crosses his fingers as his father mulls over the idea. "I suppose that is a good idea. That way you don't have to keep sending letters to him, or coming back and forth from here to the city, wasting time and possibly blowing your cover." He begins nodding as he talks seeming to talk himself into the idea. "Yes, that is a good idea Barin. That is why I assigned this job to you. You are smart. Go tell the monk to collect what things he has. I will send for your horse and second to be saddled. This..." He opens a drawer in his desk and pulls out a small pouch. "This is the money I have for you to get started. Here is a second, you will both need to try to buy new clothes to fit it. For the love of god Barin, buy a new pair of boots."

"Thank you, Father," Barin says taking the money and then bowing. "I promise that I will not disappoint you." Barin lies.

24

Paulo

"Go, I will be out here watching for the signal. This will work don't worry," Lyra says giving Paulo a little shove. "Go get your friend."

Paulo takes a step forward then another and another, gaining momentum as he gains courage. He spreads his hands out wide and mutters something in elvish. A stone spear made of a single piece or rock launches itself into his hand, and large boulders begin to spin around him as he runs. The first sentry sees him coming and barely gets out a cry before a rock goes spinning into his chest.

The next man who appears gets a shout out and Paulo can hear them all running through the camp at him. He shouts again and again in his mind hoping she will hear, that she won't block him from her mind. *Shauna where are you?*

Paulo? she asks, finally hearing him, *Paulo, what are you doing here? Get out of here! Leave.*

No he says resolutely as his stones fly at men all around him, slamming into their head, necks, arms, and chest. *I swore I would protect you and then I left you.*

I told you to go! Just like I am telling you to get out of here right now!

I left you, Shauna, we need each other! I can't leave you because I promised to protect you. I am not going to let the same thing that happened to my brother happen to you.

A guard gets through the ring of rocks and grabs at Paulo, but he slashes at him with the spear. The man flinches, and the flinch is his death. The rock hits him in the back of the head crushing his skull.

"I'm sorry to break up this little reunion, but I must cut in," Damian shouts, his voice ringing in their heads louder than an avalanche. Paulo cries out clapping his hands to his ears in pain. His ring of stones falls, and he is left unguarded.

"NO!" Shauna yells. "Paulo run!"

But he can't. Seconds after the rocks fall Damian's oily black magick wraps Paulo up and carries him through the camp like a trophy on display.

* * *

Shauna

I slump down next to the post they tied me to. I sit in the middle of the camp on display. Always on display. The little Magick Human trapped.

What had he been thinking? Did he honestly think he could save me by marching into the middle of the camp in broad daylight? I shake my head. Whatever Paulo had been doing he hadn't been thinking. He had come in strong with his boulders thudding into the soldiers, but it didn't last long. Even if he had tried to talk to me I would have told him to stay away. It was not the right moment. But would it ever be?

133

It was stupid. I let hope get to me for a moment. I felt the thrill of it fill my chest like a rushing waterfall. But then, like the water cascading away the feeling fell leaving me full of dread. I couldn't do that to myself. Push those thoughts away. If Damian didn't break me, thoughts like that would. "You have to be strong," I tell myself. "Stronger than a mountain," I think to myself.

Out of the corner of my eye, I see a familiar face peeking through the tent flaps. "Philippe?" I whisper carefully that no one else hears me "Philippe what is happening?"

He glances over at me clearly wanting to speak but unsure of himself. I look around too, but no one is paying any attention to us. Philippe hurries over and lifts me to my feet before I can move to stop him he wraps me up in a tight hug. "God Shauna, what are we going to do? I hate seeing you like this," he says looking deep into my eyes. "Why can't you just cooperate? It would save you from so much pain."

I manage to wiggle my way free and hesitate before saying, "Philippe, you know I can't do that. Do you honestly think that I am going to sit idly by, or even help these monsters to destroy all we have ever known? Because that is what they are Philippe, they are monsters plain and simple." He tries to speak, and I run over his words with my own. "They are destroying our lives as they slowly take over. They have our families locked up in cells beneath the city. Did they tell you that? They don't have just our families but anyone who didn't get away from the city. They hurt my father just to get me to talk. And you want me to join them? You expect me to ignore all of that. If you do, you don't know me."

Philippe looks almost ashamed for a moment, he won't look at me that was for sure. "Shauna, I don't agree with what they do. But you need to think about your survival."

"No, we need to think about who we are and what we believe in. I believe in my powers, my family and that everything these people do is wrong. If you agree with them okay. But we cannot speak anymore."

"Shauna please listen to me. I hate to see you get hurt."

I can't help but huff- this boy would never listen to common sense. "Get used to it, I'm sure they won't let up anytime soon. Now, where is Paulo?"

He looks away. "You have changed. Shauna, it's only been a week. I don't understand how you can act like you feel nothing."

I feel a stab of pain, this time, it is more mental pain than physical, but I still need to fight to keep my face blank.

"It was long enough. I need to be able to take care of myself. I can't waste my time on deciding whether or not I still want to be with you."

"I miss you."

I roll my eyes and walk around my post. I am trying to act like I don't care, but this is hurting. "They are questioning Paulo now," he says quietly. "I was sent away."

I stop my pacing. "Is he okay? How are they doing it?"

"I— I don't know they sent me away after—" He pauses trying to get me to look at him.

"As you said, it's only been a week so don't look at me like that." That was as close as he was going to get me to admitting I miss him. "He is my friend; he is the only person that might have an idea what this has been like for me." I look down at the ground the grass around the post has been worn down in a circle from my pacing.

"Look you— you will be okay. So will your friend. I just want to help you and be by your side. It's just hard right now."

I glare at him. "Maybe soon it will be more convenient for you," I snap turning away and walking as far as the cords will let me.

I see him reaching for me out of the corner of my eye when Damian's voice rips through the air. "Philippe step away from that girl if you know what's good for you." Philippe jumps back like a trained dog.

"Where is Paulo?" I snap disgusted by everything around me.

Damian looks off to the side and nods. Paulo is thrust forward by soldiers, he stays up for a moment before crumbling to the ground. He doesn't look like he is in rough shape. Nothing like I am sure I do. He has few bruises on his arms and chest, a black eye and a split lip, and like me a slice on his arm from the truth blade. "He is just like you. Manipulative with his words."

I start to open my mouth to release a snappy comeback when a coil of oily magick floats a little closer. On that cue, I snap my jaws shut. "Hmmm, it seems as if we might be learning something." I swear if I weren't tied up– this man, this monster, this thing, would have a harder time standing there over top of me. "What is it pet? What empty threat do you want to try and throw at me this time?" Damian asks kicking Paulo in the chest knocking the wind out of him before stepping on his stomach on his way over to me.

I glare at him, picturing water coming up, flowing out of the ground, flowing up his legs, spilling into his mouth. I would pour it in his eyes, his mouth, his nose, in his ears. He would cough and splutter and gag. I would drown him. I would flood his lungs so no air would ever fill his lungs. I would watch his face turn red, then blue as he tried to force the water from his body.

"What? Nothing to say? You shock me."

"I have things to say, believe me. I just know how to play my cards."

"Oh do you? You don't seem to have the winning hand right now."

I look down at Paulo as he is gasping for air. I glance up at Damian "So you have us? Now, what will you do with us?" I probe feeding Damian something so he would keep talking.

"Oh you know, you should have guessed by now. We will create our own Frituals. We will match you. I am only keeping you right now because of the information each of you has."

Damian continues talking about a dark set of Frituals.

Get ready. Paulo mouths.

Get ready? Get ready for what? I think. He closes his eyes for a moment, and when he opens them they flash a deeper green for a moment. *Now, we are going now.*

Damian glances around, a vibration seems to buzz through the air. "What is that?" Damian asks glancing around. He looks at us, a glint of fear in his eyes as we all recognize the buzz of energy from someone casting. "Stop. Stop that," he snaps.

"That isn't us," I say, just as confused as him. Who is casting? Is it Philippe? He hasn't done anything since he had dissolved the water whip.

"I don't believe you."

"You know it isn't us. It's too far from us; you would have known the moment we embraced any magick." Paulo coughs, sitting up behind Damian.

"Then who is?" Damian snaps, pushing him aside. "You! Find Philippe, now get him from his tent."

The soldiers, distracted by their commander for a moment, don't look at us as the run after Damian. Paulo stands up slowly then hurries to my side. "We are getting out of here," he whispers hurriedly in my ear as his fingers fumble with the ropes binding my hands together.

"But how? You do realize that we are directly in the middle of their camp right?"

"Someone has gained an attitude since you have been here haven't you?" I don't answer "Okay, okay that person out there is a friend. I will explain later. There, just hold the cord like this," he says, lightly wrapping the cord back around my wrists and placing the end in my hand. "They will think you're still tied up. Be ready to run." He lies back down on the ground pretending to be in pain again.

Philippe comes running over. "Hurry Shauna, I know you are planning something. Run, get away, this place is terrible and I hate seeing you here." He takes a knife and slices the rope nicking my skin. "Ah I'm sorry, I am rushing. You need to leave. Get a head start."

I rub my wrist where the blade nicked me. "No, it's fine. Thank you, now you be careful. I can't imagine Damian will be happy with you for doing this." I look at his face for a moment unmarked by a ceremony but bruised by the people I was leaving him to.

I glance at Paulo. "Shauna... I know what you are thinking, but we need to get going—"

"We will need him, Paulo, he might be fire. My ceremony."

"What— fine we will figure all this out when we get to safety." I nod and we start to run. A gale is starting up as we are talking, pulling the tent lines taught, causing them to pull and lean. "This way." The three of us move heads down avoiding the eyes of all we pass. When we reach the edge of the tent line, we pause.

"Where are we going?" I ask Paulo.

Before he is answered, a voice cries out, "Shauna stop, that's not me." I whip around to see Philippe running at us flanked by two guards. "That's Damian," he shouts, flinching as two boulders take out the guards to the left and right.

It takes about five seconds for me to process that there are two Phillippe's. I glance back and forth between the two. "Well seeing as lover boy blew my cover," Philippe-Damian growls, "I might as well stop you here." He fashions a black blade, bringing it down into my wrist as a boulder whizzes by, missing him by inches. It flips back around and nails him in the chest.

I am trying to stumble away; this isn't an actual blade. Once it makes contact with my skin, it slides in melting with my arm, burning red hot. "I— what the hell. Go, go move." I can feel the fire seeping under my skin I look down and see black veins like what had covered Damian's skin spreading across mine. "Paulo, he poisoned me. I—"

My world is moving, undulating like a child carrying a large glass of water. I feel my legs start to give out. I see Philippe's face swim into my peripheral vision. I try to fight, to get away. Is he real? "Hey, hey it's me, it's me," Philippe says trying to get a better grip on me as I slip to the ground, my world fading away for the second time in a week.

25

Barin

Barin swings his leg over his horse's back and lands with a soft thud. The inside of his legs are sore from riding, he is going to be walking bow-legged for the next few days.

Alois is worse. Months of sitting and occasionally pacing around his cell have left his legs weak, the muscles slowly disintegrating. He nearly falls when he dismounts, his legs giving out from underneath him. "Whoa," Alois says pulling himself up with the horse's saddle, "I need to get used to that again."

Barin smiles and takes Alois' horse from him so the other elf can go sit down. "I am sure we can do some riding to get used to it. Unless you would prefer to walk all over the city." Alois doesn't respond; he just hobbles over to sit on a bench in the middle of the yard outside the inn, where Nurzan had rented out apartments for Barin. "Do you want to go check in or would you rather that I did it after we get the horses situated?"

Alois looks at the building then at the barn. "It would probably be best if we went in together."

A stable boy comes up and stares as he takes the horse

from him. Barin tosses him a coin and walks over to Alois. "Remember I am not meant to be a Dark One right now to let me get close to people. I am meant to be me. On top of that, I am already going to have enough of an issue being stared at because of how I look, I don't need people staring or worse running away from me because of who my father is. Come on let's get settled," Barin says slinging his bag over his shoulder. The inn his father has chosen is not fancy by any means, it is perfect for this sort of thing, no one will suspect this place. It has faded oak planks that have a few torches mounted on the outside to light the inn at night.

They make their way into the room and look around the pub. Barin walks up to the counter and sits down waiting for the bartender to notice them. Barin waves the man down, and the barkeeper comes over, leaning against the counter. "What can I do for you two gentlemen?" the man asks wiping off the bar with a cloth that needed to be washed yesterday.

Barin looks at the man- he is skinny, most of the bartenders that Barin had ever met were always on the rounder side like they snuck food and drinks all the time while on the job. This bartender is lean but robust. The kind of man that wouldn't need another man to help him if a fight broke out in his tavern. "Hello, my name is Barin, I have an apartment reserved here, is it available now?"

"Ah, Master Barin, I'm glad you made it this morning. I hope that you will be pleased with the accommodations." He comes around the bar and shakes Barin's hand.

"I am eager to see these rooms as well. I have heard good things about them. You run a tight ship. Master?" Barin asks.

"Jansen, master Jansen. I try to keep my rooms in the best conditions, I don't often hear bad things," he says leading Barin and Alois down the hall.

The hall is made of the same oak paneling from outside on the bottom of the hall and with dark blue paint on the top. It makes the hall feel dark but comfortable. Jansen turns at the second door on the left and opens the door to a staircase. "Your apartments are on the top floor, so you don't have the need to worry about being bothered by neighbors. One of the perks of having my apartments." He opens the door and leads the two into the room.

Barin nods, in acknowledgment, he is too busy scanning the room that he would be staying in for the next few weeks. It is large, but he notices that it feels slightly cramped with the furniture that is in it. He can tell what the standard furniture of the room is and what is newly added with the knowledge that there was going to be a second inhabitant of the room. There is one large wardrobe at the end of the room with a bed next to it pressed into the corner, and a second smaller bed mirroring the first on the opposite side of the room. The beds each have their own trunk at the end of the bed. A porcelain pitcher and bowl on a washstand near the door, with a coat rack next to it. "Thank you, Mr. Jansen."

"You're welcome Master Barin. I will leave you to it. If you need anything else, I will be downstairs," Jansen says with a small bow before leaving, closing the door as he leaves.

"Well, Alois what do you think?" Barin asks moving into the room and dropping his bag on the bed.

"I think that the bed over there looks very nice. It is calling my name, I need to rest my legs a bit," Alois says dropping onto the bed with a sigh. "I am feeling it now, and I will probably be feeling it again tomorrow as well," he says pulling his boots off and massaging his ankles. "What are you planning to get done today?"

Barin leans back against his pillows. "As much as I would like to rest as well, I feel like I need to begin exploring the city. It isn't the city I know anymore." He feels a hint of sadness creeping into his voice, it was something that he was going to have to suppress while he was here. He was here on a job, even if it was one he didn't want to do. Barin wouldn't be surprised if his father would have assigned a man or two to watch his progress. He knew that the idea of being able to just track down a man or woman that had not yet been tested would be slim to none. "Can I borrow your map?" he asks sitting back up.

"Of course," Alois says, reaching into a bag and pulling out a folded bit of parchment. Barin unfolds the map of the city, it has the original ink markings all over it but also with charcoal markings that Alois has made all over it to represent the places that he has been to.

"Thank you, I will be back in a few hours," he says rising from the bed. Barin digs into his bag and pulls out a knife and slips it under his belt. "I want to see the city, my city," he says making his way toward the door.

"Don't let the changes get to you too much."

Barin nods and heads out the door and down the stairs. He heads back out toward the bar and then moves out to the courtyard again. He sees that the horses have been taken care of - their two heads hanging over their stall doors. He follows the lane back around the outside of the inn, Barin looks down at the map in his hand. Left or right, which way should he start? Right, he will go right.

Barin wants to find his childhood home. He wants to find the last place his mother had been seen. He wants to get lost in the city and never return to his father's side in that dark castle on the hill.

The road is dirty, puddles of brown sludge on the sides of the road are hard to avoid when people press their way through on horseback not caring if they take people out. "Who's that guy?" Barin asks one small woman on the side of the road when the two of them are nearly taken out by a wagon wheel.

The woman adjusts her headscarf then spits on the sidewalk. "Dark Ones. You would think that they would leave now. They had done enough, but no- this seems to be their new base. That castle on the outside of the city. It used to belong to our king, but they just killed him and then replaced him with their 'higher rule.' An oppressive tyranny is what I would call it, but what would I know?" She huffs. She is dirty, the amount of grime that cakes her body is like a second skin. Barin wishes he could do something to comfort this woman who seems lost in her own city.

"This used to be my home," he says. "My father took me away when everything happened. This is my first time back."

"Why would you come back? You were probably better off where you were, anywhere is better than here," she replies, bitterness staining her voice. She adjusts her headscarf again, making sure that it lies just right against her head, gives Barin another once over then leaves, making sure to avoid the puddles that now stain the bottom of her dress.

Barin turns down another road to his right that seems not to get as much foot traffic. He realizes why fairly quickly. Down here the torch light doesn't seem to penetrate the darkness as well, the sadness that hangs in the air like fog, clouding the vision of all there. The filth he had narrowly avoided before is now everywhere, he can feel it soaking into the cracks in his boots. Bodies lean up against the walls cringing away from him as he walks. The old women from before seemed spotless compared to some of these people.

"Sir," a shy little boy asks tugging on his sleeve. "Do you have any spare coins?" He puts his dirty hands out expectantly. Apparently this boy was used to people who wandered down here giving up their coin at the sign of his dirty little body.

Barin shakes his head. "I'm sorry lad, I don't have anything for you." He begins turning out his pockets, with each bunch of fabric that comes up empty the child's shoulders slump a bit more and more. "I am poor as well. I spent all of my money to come back here. To get away from the dangers I had at home, I need to find a job." The boy nods, understanding that they both are in the same struggle. He wanders away looking for a new target to get coinage off of.

Barin feels the coins in his breast pocket burning like a hot poker on his chest. His father's notebook had warned him that the poor in the city were desperate with their begging. He had made sure to remind Barin to always keep any money he carried on him in the breast pocket of jackets to avoid being pickpocketed. He continues down the road past the other beggars. They had all watched when the boy approached and since seeing that he wasn't a worthy target, turn their eyes elsewhere as well.

Barin pulls out his map at a street corner and glances at the sign comparing it to his map. He isn't far now. He turns down a road on his right moving back toward where the people move faster and have places to go. He picks up his own pace hoping to use their momentum to mask him.

26

Philippe

Shauna goes limp in his arms after he tells her he is the real Philippe. One arm hangs around his shoulders, and he has his other arm half around her waist. He freezes and looks at Paulo. "If you are real, we will need you. I know right now she isn't sure she can trust you. I don't know if I can trust you. But to be honest, I don't have a choice. I will have to take your word that you won't betray us."

Philippe adjusts the limp Shauna, so she is easier to carry. She was like a baby with her head on his chest. "I will not betray you. I can't betray her; I only did what I did because I had been taken. The spell was broken when you punched through their defenses. I haven't gone through what the two have. I have had something different. I am with you."

"Then let's go, we need to get out of here. We need to get to somewhere safe where we can take care of her. Head toward that end of the field, I will back you up."

Philippe takes off as quickly as he can without bumping Shauna around. He has to go a few different directions around the field as little tornadoes swirl across escaping the tent city. Philippe tries to ignore the screams he is hearing as people fly twenty feet into the air and thud to the ground as they are blown away.

"So," Philippe asks, "who is this person we are meeting?" He pauses for a second as he adjusts Shauna in his arms.

Paulo looks over his shoulder for a second at the camp, but no one seems to be following the trio. "Her name is Lyra, she is the Apieto Fritual." He glances at the blank face Philippe has as he tries to translate the word. Exasperated Paulo points back at the tents "Air. She can control the wind," he says shortly. Philippe looks away pretending to survey the tent line. *Isn't it a little obvious?* he thinks as a gust of wind ruffles his hair.

"Do you think that we can trust her?" Philippe asks. After a short moment, he realizes how stupid that must have sounded. "Oh— you uh you probably can trust her more than me at this moment." An awkward silence follows this statement that Paulo does not confirm nor deny. But that is confirmation enough. *How can I get them to trust me?* He looks down at the girl in his arms. *How can you ever forgive me?* he asks, thinking of all the times he and Shauna had snuck out and gone down to the lake to look up at the stars. Or the times where they had gone into little side alleys and hoped nobody would look.

One time they had met at three in the afternoon when they each had gotten out of classes. They made excuses to parents saying, "I'm just going to be at the library, I got a note about a new book." And "I told Geoffrey I would help him get some of his chores done today." They had met at this stone about a mile away from the town. Well, that was where they said they would meet. They made it about a quarter of the way there. Then they darted into the woods. Shauna would hike up her skirts to an indecent height so that the sticks wouldn't catch and tear it as they moved through the woods. And he would 'scout ahead.' It was like they were on an adventure.

In a little notebook, Shauna always kept with her they slowly mapped out their side of the lake. They found old farms and the skeletons of old cows and horses. They made a big loop that passed the battle-scarred ground where the skeletons of men and elves still in armor lay. Their breasts pierced by arrow or sword. A piece of physical history.

They were going to explore a section of the forest they had looked toward but never actually ventured to. It was across a broad gully, and for a time they hadn't been able to find a way across. It was too far to jump, and there were no human-made bridges. But, after the last storm a tree had fallen across, so Philippe had cut away some of the branches that would hinder their passage, and now they were ready. "Are you sure this is a good idea?" Shauna had asked sitting on the tree and bouncing slightly to test its strength. It held.

"We don't have to do this. We can explore elsewhere," he replied.

"No! No, I want to do it," she rushed. "I—I just wanted to make sure that you know that you wanted to do it."

He laughed- this was what she would do. She wouldn't admit to him that she was scared. Instead, she would sort of nudge around the point but ultimately would talk herself into it. "I don't know, it is at least a fifteen-foot drop," he said peering over the edge.

"What, are you scared now? Big baby." She stuck her tongue out at him.

"Oh really. Well then, if you are so brave, what if I make you go first?" he goaded flashing a smile.

Shauna froze, gears working in her head as she tried to come up with an answer to hide her fear. "But if I go first who will scout? I need to watch and take care of you remember."

"Ooooh," he laughed, "is that how this works?" With Shauna, he didn't have to hide behind the rough exterior. He could laugh, and joke around, and just be happier.

"Yes, yes it is," she said. "Now go on. You told me on the way over here that you were going to show me just how it was done. So let's see."

"Alright then," he grinned jumping up on to the bark. If he was honest, he was a little bit nervous. It had rained earlier that morning, but the sun had dried the tree down for the most part. "Here I go," he said just a bit less confident. He took his first step testing each movement before committing to it and putting down his full weight.

"Philippe," a voice calls breaking him out of the memories. "Philippe come on in here. This is the place. Just keep walking that way, you will see a small fire pit. Lyra and I will be there soon. I just want to block off the entrance once she gets here."

"You want to trap us in here?"

"Well yeah. I would rather be stuck in the mountain than exposed to them."

Philippe, knowing Paulo is right and there is no point in trying to argue, just continues down the path. It doesn't take long for Philippe to find the circle of stones with the dark ashes in the middle. He carefully bends down and lays Shauna on the ground.

He looks over at the fire circle and the pile of branches and blackened wood. He hasn't done any magick since he had vaporized the water whip Shauna had first created. He crouches next to the fire circle and touches a finger to the edge of one log. He focuses his energy into a single stream, and still had a moment of surprise as the small flame pops to light. The flame flickers for a moment then transfers to the log, popping and snapping as it grows to life.

"Oh good, you started a fire," a girl's voice says from behind Philippe. He turns to see the owner walking with Paulo.

"Uh, yeah I thought it would be a good thing to have," he says awkwardly standing up and moving to the side.

"How is she?" Paulo asks trying to get a glimpse of Shauna past Philippe.

"I don't know," Philippe mutters. The veins on Shauna's body stand out like someone has taken a quill and ink and traced every line.

"We need to get her help," the girl says.

"Yes we do. I am Philippe, I am the fire Fritual. Are you the air Fritual?"

She nods, "My name is Lyra."

"Lyra, what can we do?" She and Paulo look at each other for a moment. "Look I know you don't trust me yet. But I don't want her to be hurt any more than she is now. And to do that we need to do something. So let's make a plan."

"There is one place we could take her. We will have to go straight through this mountain. We can't go outside, they have us surrounded. Damian's men used up a lot of energy to summon quite a few demons to patrol all over the mountain."

"So where is this place we think we should go to?" Philippe asks. "Why do you seem unsure of this?"

Paulo glances at Lyra then goes on. "You see the Dark Ones have taken over so much of the kingdoms that even if we go there we might not be safe. The people that could help would not be able to protect us. We would be all on our own."

"These elves take a vow of peace. They do not attack; they take no sides, they only heal."

"Ok, so we just need to be on our guard. Right?"

"Well yes but—"

"Look we don't really have a lot of time for buts."

"Their methods are old but faithful."

"No offense but we need the best people we can get. Shauna was just poisoned by Dark One magick. It isn't going to be an easy fix, and we are not going to have a lot of time."

"Fine but I warned you about it okay?" Lyra says.

Philippe doesn't understand why it is such a big deal. He will do whatever it takes to make sure that Shauna would be ok. "When will we go?"

"Let's rest for a few minutes then head out," Paulo says. "Lyra would you mind putting the fire out for us? It was a good idea, but I don't want them tracking us through the smoke," Paulo says pointing at the smoke hole in the roof. Lyra nods, looked over at flames, and a breeze stirs in the cave spiraling up before coming down and snuffing out the fire.

27

Shauna

The three take turns carrying me through the mountain. Philippe and Paulo pass me back and forth to give each other a break, Lyra moves me on a cushion of air in front of her as they walk around the tunnel that Paulo had sent before them. Paulo sets the dirt to open in front of them and cycle behind them and fill in behind them so there would be a solid wall of earth between them and the Dark Ones at all times.

I hear bits of conversations but for the most part, the three stay quiet, or I had gone in and out of consciousness too much to follow a real conversation. I am in so much pain; I can feel the black magick as it forces its way through my body.

There is a soft rumble as the earth finally opens up on the other side. The light that comes through is beautiful but also painful, stabbing my eyes. "Mmmm" I groan, the sound coming out before I can stop myself.

"Oh Shauna, we will be there soon," Paulo murmurs shifting my head, so my face is in the darkness of his shoulder a bit more. "It is only a half mile or so, it might just be a bit harder to be safe." The world is harsh in its light. I just want to turn and hide, but I feel so heavy. The world feels like it is pressing down on my chest. "Lyra are we clear, how does it look up there?" Paulo asks looking up into the sky.

"Wh—who is Lyra?" I mumble trying to look up and around, but my head just flops over because it weighs too much.

"Lyra is our new friend, you will meet her when you are better. Don't talk too much, just rest, keep your energy up."

My eyes swim as I try to focus on the blur that moves through the sky. "Is she?"

"Yes, she is safe. She is someone we need, you can meet her personally later. Now rest," he says gently. The world continues to fade in and out as we travel. I can't feel my body. The pain is gone. I feel like I am floating around the world. My eyelids feel like they are leaden with a dozen anvils. Each eyelash drags downward by the sheer force of gravity.

"Lyra do you think this is a good idea?"

"It is our only option. We will just have to be persuasive."

"Why do we have to be persuasive?" Philippe asks.

"Well," Paulo says, "we aren't quite sure that this will actually work with you being human rather than elves."

"So um? Well, don't get annoyed please but uh— ok just how old are you?" Philippe asks trying really hard no be insulting but letting his curiosity get the better of him.

"I am three hundred and seven," Lyra says.

"And I am, two hundred and forty-seven," replies Paulo.

If I could have spoken at that moment, I probably would have made a sputtering sound very similar to the one that escapes Philippe's lips. "You can't be serious."

The two elves share a grin "Yes, we are, Philippe. Now the people we are going to see are much, much older. These elves demand a high amount of respect." Lyra stops the procession down the mountain. "I have been here once, just promise me that you won't talk unless you are spoken to directly. If you are, please, please, think through what you are going to say before you do so."

"I will do my best," Philippe says in a somber tone I have rarely heard. "So what do we do?"

"As I said I have been here before, so I will go first. You stay here with Paulo. I will come back for you shortly. Then we will go from there." Before anyone can question what she means she slinks off into the night.

Philippe and Paulo are silent for a few minutes as they wait in the dark for Lyra to return. "So what is it like?" Philippe asks.

"What is what like?" Paulo asks crossing his arms and leaning up against a tree.

"Well, what is it like to live so long?"

Paulo pauses to think "Well I guess it isn't much different than for humans, in a societal sense. You aren't considered to have matured into an adult until you have reached a certain age correct?"

Philippe puts me down gently at his feet, resting my head lightly on a log, for a pillow. "Yeah, when you turn seventeen you are somehow suddenly able to choose the ways to run your life, even though the day before when you were sixteen you weren't."

Paulo gives a small snort that I assume is accompanied by a little smile. "It is about the same for us. However, it isn't seventeen. For us, it is around one hundred."

"One hundred... So to the people we are going to for help, Shauna and I will seem like infants. We are little mewling babies."

Paulo laughs again, but this time it sounds a little bit more awkward. "Yes. That is why, though you may have reached maturity for your people, in the eyes of my people you really need to prove your worth. That you can handle yourself. Most of all that you deserve the title of Fritual."

Philippe takes a deep breath exhaling and blowing out his lips. "How do I try to convince someone I am meant to do something that I still can't believe happened to me?"

"That my friend is something that you will have to find within yourself."

28

Lyra

The murmured voices of Philippe and Paulo fade as Lyra moves down the mountain closer to the stone building hidden at the bottom of the hill. One of the large windows lets out the soft golden light of candles onto the ground outside. Illuminating her path through the trees as she draws near to it.

Lyra kneels in front of the large oak door and gives it four sharp knocks. She then bends her head and laces her fingers in her lap, and waits for the door to open. She does not move when she hears the soft pad of the elf to the door, or when his shadow falls on her as he looks out at her through the window, nor does she move when the door creaks open. These people are all about tradition and ritual. Should you break it, they would not be as willing to help the group.

"Rise, my child." Lyra stands but keeps her head and eyes down. "Why have you come to me, my child?"

"My friend is gravely ill. She has been poisoned by the hand of darkness. I fear for her."

"How did this come to be?"

"She was kidnapped, and during our rescue, she was poisoned."

The elf pauses mulling over this information. "Why was she kidnapped?"

Lyra slowly looks up at him exposing the soft yellow spirals on her skin. "Because she is like me. We are the Frituals. She is the Aka Fritual."

"My child where is your friend?" He gasps "Why did you not bring her straight here?"

Lyra looks back down. "Because she is human. I didn't want her and my companions to use up the energy if you cannot help her. But you and your home were the closest that could save her."

The elf pauses, and a shadow falls over his face.

"The girl is still on the mountain, I came down alone. My friends do not know where I have gone. I beg of you to help her. Is not having the name of Fritual bestowed upon you not legitimizing? Do this not mean she has the honor of our people?"

Again, the man pauses. "Do we know her ancestry? As you say she has been blessed with the name of Fritual, but I must ask as a healer for some of our methods will not work on a child of man."

It doesn't take Lyra long to form an answer. "No, there has not been a moment to talk about home and what it was like before or what the future holds."

"Then we will go forward with caution, we will test the waters carefully. Fetch your friend. You have spoken with confidence and wisdom. You have done well by your title as Fritual."

Lyra bows deeply until her braid falls over her shoulder. "Thank you so much for your kindness and giving spirit. I will be back with my friend in a short time. Again many, many thanks." Lyra turns and speeds through the night back to her friends, praying that she wouldn't be too late.

29

Philippe

"I will guide you down the mountain now," Lyra says after gently lifting Shauna up on a pillow of air.

Paulo looks over at her. "How did you learn about this place Lyra?"

Lyra pauses staring hard into the woods in front of her. Shauna drops a few inches as Lyra's concentration is broken. Memories crash through her mind in waves. "I, it's hard. It was my family. My brother brought me here. He was sick too." The words stutter from her lips.

Paulo puts a hand on her shoulder. "Please, I understand."

She takes a deep calming breath. "No, I should tell my story. It might help me, I have been alone for a long time. Maybe once we get settled." She turns to Philippe "Do you happen to know if Shauna has any Elven in her? Her father or her mother?"

Philippe laughs. "Her father is most definitely not Elven. But her mother might have had some Elven blood. She was an elegant woman; she had the "Elven look" but in a way that some would call flawed."

"How was she flawed?" Lyra asks.

"Well where your skin is clear skin, hers had a light splash of freckles across her nose. Her hair was like Shauna's pale gold, but it had a more brassy tone to it."

"I see," says Paulo. "She had the beauty of our race but the softer beauty of man."

"Yes, she was a beautiful woman. Why do you ask?"

Lyra pauses while she guides the trio around a tree and some brambles. "Some of the methods our people use are very dangerous for the race of man. The wrong herbs could kill her."

Philippe stops short in his tracks. "Is this wise?"

"They are our only hope. Come on, wc need to hurry. They are expecting her." They walk on in silence, hurrying along, ignoring the tug of branches and brambles that tug at their clothing.

Slowly the lights come into view. "Lyra, are we here?"

"Yes, my son," the elder elf says. Philippe bows low following Lyra's actions. "My children, before we can begin I must remind you that you must never speak of this place. We are a place of peace and solitude separate from the rest of the world. I would not want the chaos of the world to taint this place."

Philippe and Paulo nod. "If I may ask, sir." Philippe asks. The elf nodded. "What makes this place so special? Is it some holy ground?"

The elf pauses in the doorway and looks at the trio deciding whether or not they are worthy of learning the true significance of the place. The patterns on the faces of the other three prove that they did. "He was born here. The one who started all of this."

Paulo freezes as he steps over the threshold. "You mean Matron. Matron was born here."

"Yes, my son. The elf who is your ancestor who you derived

your powers from, the last of the Frituals, was born in this cottage. He lived here for a time before moving to Cabineral Lake for his training." He turns to Philippe. "Our people are very different. We do not have as many children nearly as often as you. For us, each birth is a special blessing. For some these places of birth are considered holy. This cottage, in particular, represents so much more than just a birth of one Elven child. But one who would start the road to an age of peace between our two races."

Philippe bows low. "I now understand the full import of this place. Thank you for sharing this with me." He stands and pauses before continuing. "Sir, if I may ask one more question. May we know your name?"

"I am Amicus. Now hurry, let's get your friend inside." Amicus put a hand under Shauna's neck and the other under her knees. He lifts her off the cushion of air Lyra had held together, and it flies away in a small breeze. Amicus carries Shauna in like she weighs nothing. Philippe takes in the simplicity of the space. It is furnished with thin wooden furniture and a few pillows. The dark wood seems to absorb all of the light from the lanterns placed around the cottage. The soft muted glow is welcoming, putting Philippe into a sense of safety causing a level of trust to begin to grow.

"Amicus? What will you do to help Shauna?" Paulo asks.

Amicus lays Shauna down on the table in the middle of the room propping her head up on a pillow. She groans. "Don't worry child. It will stop soon." He turns to the three onlookers after thoroughly examining the black gauge in Shauna's arm. "We will start with small infusions of herbs, these should help to dislodge the poisonous matter."

"Wait, Amicus, do you know what this poison is? Or what it

does?" Lyra asks.

Amicus moves to a side table covered in small jars with a myriad of herbs, and a mortar and pestle made of dark stone. He takes several leaves from three pots and begins crushing them together. He keeps working with his left hand as with his right he checks Shauna's slowing pulse. "It causes the blood to clot and solidifies in the body. If these are not dissolved soon, and we try to move her or, she moves, it could cause her veins to crack and splinter. Any blood that is still managing to flow through would cause internal bleeding." He stops mixing and grabs a small cup. "My child, I think that you can still hear me. I have made a drink that should help you. It will taste horrid. It might bring you some pain, but it is by no means intentional. I just do not know how much of our medicines your body can take."

Amicus watches for any sign of response. After a long drawn out pause, Shauna's lips part ever so slightly letting out a low rattling breath. "Okay." The sound is a sigh that tears at Philippe's heart.

"Alright my dear, we will now begin." Amicus gently tips the small wooden cup against her lips depositing the greenish-brown sludge into her mouth. As if in slow motion her face contorts in disgust as she swallows the ghastly concoction.

"It will take a few minutes to take effect. When it does, we will begin chafing her arms and legs to get the blood circulating again. If that doesn't work, she may have to drink more, or we may have to bleed her. Perhaps that can help get some of the blockages free."

Philippe pauses, his mouth open ready to speak but Lyra's words to hold his tongue echo in his mind. He glances at the two hoping that one of them will speak on his behalf. Paulo looks like he wants to speak up as well but he also remains silent. Philippe stares at Shauna lying on this thin table. She is so unkempt compared to what he knows and remembers of her. It is easy to see her as she always had been. Her hair is frizzy, and chunks are falling out of what had been at one point a neat braid. The linen sheath she had worn under her dress is stained with mud, blood, and sweat.

It had only been a few days since they had both jumped in the lake. Just a few days since he had given her a ring, just a few days since she'd given it back. Just a few days since he put the bright red blister on her arm. She had done so much in the last week. She was strong. Stronger than his father thought she was. If only he could see her now. He would never have doubted that she was a powerful woman. He steps closer to her and brushes a few sticky strands away from her dirt-streaked face. The veins he can see on the surface of her skin aren't the soft muted blue anymore, but a harsh grey-black against her pale skin. "Amicus?" Philippe whispers. "Amicus would putting her in water make her stronger?" he asks looking at her lips, cracked and flaking. It is like she is drying from the inside out. The black veins outlining where she would crack like porcelain.

"That might just help," the elf concedes after mulling the thought over in his mind. "I will go fill a tub with water. You go and start to try chafing her wrists and ankles."

Philippe takes her hand and begins rubbing where her hand met her wrist in small circular motions. Her fingers are stiff and cold. It is very disconcerting. It makes it feel like she is already dead. Not already. She isn't going to die. Under his hand, he can feel the skin slowly beginning to warm.

"She will be okay," Lyra murmurs from down by Shauna's ankle.

Philippe nods, his throat feels too thick to speak. He doesn't want to lose her again. *But did you get her back?* The little voice says in the back of his mind. He forces the voice away; he doesn't want to listen to him. They would talk about how things were when she woke up.

"Philippe stop!" Paulo says pushing Philippe away from Shauna. Philippe is shocked. Why would Paulo shove him away like that? Then he sees his hands. Small flames dance along his fingertips. His eyes jump to Shauna's red, raw skin. The previous burn he had given her on her shoulder was just beginning to fade. Now she has a matching burn on the other side.

"I, I just," he splutters.

"Philippe," Amicus says following two elves who carried in a bathtub filled with water. "Your powers are most strongly linked to your emotions. You must always be wary of them. But at this moment they can be of some use. I can put a salve on that burn later. But I need your fire now. This water is from the river." Philippe reaches out to touch it, the water hisses for a moment, but the water wins, and the flame on his finger is put out, and cold soaks his skin. "You see I fear that putting her in the cold water will help to solidify her blood. But if the water was warm? We do not have time to boil each pot individually."

"I can't control it," Philippe interrupts. "I could burn down this whole building."

"Have you ever tried to focus your power, my son?"

"Well, no but..."

"Try. If it fails, we have a whole tub of water here."

Philippe shrugs but still doesn't feel confident at all.

"Focus on heating the surface of the water. I will stir." Amicus holds up a large wooden spoon most likely used to stir big soup pots. "We can circulate the water and then help her."

Philippe nods and glances over at Shauna lying so still on the table. He takes a deep breath and focuses in on one finger. His index finger. He feels heat flow down his arm, his wrist, his hand and into the very tip of his finger. A small flame pops to light. It grows and grows until his whole hand is a flickering ball of intense heat. He shifts his weight and slips his hand under the surface of the water with a loud sizzle. The flames are put out instantly, but he keeps forcing heat out through his hand into the water until the water starts to stir on its own, tiny bubbles floating away from his hand.

Amicus touches the tip of the water with his finger. "Perfect Philippe, please go rest now, you will need it."

Philippe feels the weight of the magick fall on him in waves. His body feels like it is the tub with all the water pressing down on his chest. As he slumps down beside the tub the other three gently lower Shauna into the water. "Please let this work," he mutters before falling into a deep sleep.

30

Taytra

Taytra paces back and forth across the floor. She counts as she walks. Six steps one way, six steps the other way. She pauses at the end of her current patrol to stop and stare at the man across the hall. "What was the point of this, we were fine as we were," she gestures to the empty cell around her. In the night when they were peacefully sleeping, well as peacefully as one can sleep on a pile of hay, guards came to take away her father and Moraine. There had been no warning, no reason to suspect that something was to happen.

"Where are they?" Taytra snaps. The guard continues to look off into space, completely ignoring her. His helmet covers his face so she can't see any expression from him. "Listen to me! Where are they?" She grabs the bars getting as close as she can. "Answer me!"

The guard glances in her direction. "I wouldn't do that if I were you," he says and then turns away.

"Why?" She looks at her hands and sees the black coils leaving the point where the locking spell had been placed. "What the?" She steps back and watches with a mixture of fear and fascination as the coils break and float towards her.

"I told you," says the guard. His eyes flicker towards her for a moment.

"Help me," she says trying desperately not to be backed into a corner.

"I can't."

"Yes, you can. Just open the door and come in here," she demands, fear gaining an edge in her voice.

The guard turns to her, the facade of disinterest starting to fail. "Taytra, I do wish I could help, but they have my family. If I help you then..." The guard pulls off his helmet, his face full of earnest desire and a plea for sympathy. He stops as the sound of running feet comes down the hall.

The guard steps back, his face falling back into the mask of disinterest as he slips his helmet back on.

Boiling anger floods Taytra at the sight of her sister's friend, and she grips the bars harder.

"Ward, what is going on here? Why did the alarm go off?"

Ward snaps to attention, his hands flat against his sides. "Sir, my watch is still quite agitated after having been separated."

"How else would you expect me to react? Where the hell are-" She ends her sentence with a yelp as the coils wraps around her wrists pulling them to her waist. "Please stop this."

Ward continues as though Taytra has never interrupted him. "As you can see, there is no need for alarm. She is not going anywhere."

The officer nods. "Good, keep up the good work; I will find someone to switch with you soon, your watch is almost up."

Ward nods. "It is an honor to serve those who will bring back what is right." He bows low, his right hand crossed over his chest. He stays bent until the officer's footsteps fade away.

"How do I get this thing off me?" Taytra asks struggling in

her cell as she tries desperately to grab the edge of the coil. "Damn it Ward, you better tell me. If your father knew what you were doing!"

Ward steps close to the bars tossing his helmet to the floor. "My father already knows. I have had to guard his cell twice already. Damn it, Taytra, this isn't my choice!" He rubs his hands over his face. "Okay stop, stop struggling." When she struggles more he hisses, "Taytra stop!" She freezes. "It will keep winding around you more and more until you can't move if you keep struggling like that. The moment it senses that you have stopped struggling it will begin to fall away slowly. The coils are made of magick; they are 'designed' if you will, to feel the emotions of their captive."

"Where did you hear this nonsense?" she asks taking deep breaths trying not to move as the coil creeps up her shoulder.

"I learned it from them. When they took me, they taught me their ways. I learned their commands and the proper signs of respect. I learned their hierarchy and a great many more things. So please relax, you will be free soon."

Taytra fixes on the smooth cadence in his voice. This makes sense, and as he speaks, she realizes it could be quite useful. "How much would you say you know about them?" The first of the coils falls off her skin.

"Enough to get by without a possible thrashing," he replies.

"How about you get me out of here, and we can get together, we can get our families out together." The coils start floating back to the alarm disk on the door.

"And how the hell will that work? You saw what happened when you touched the alarm, they will know instantly."

"What about Omar?"

Ward winces. "My father. I want to say he will be alright, but

Tay, he can't help in a rebellion."

"No, but others will. What is happening isn't right. As far as I can tell none of you boys want to be doing this."

"No, there are a few bastards that think this will help them. But by the Goddess, I hope not.

Taytra sits down and begins to sketch out a crude floor plan on the cell floor. "Well, then let's get to planning and figure out a way to get those out that deserve it."

31

Barin

Barin rushes along the busy road, the poor bumping into him as he goes. "Hey watch it," one says after they bump into Barin. He just nods and continues to the end of the road back to the inn. As per usual Mr. Jansen waves at him as he comes through the door but Barin just shakes his head and continued down the hall to his room. Barin knocks lightly on the door before coming into his room. Alois sits on the bed, head buried in a book. "You know you can come out of the inn. No one is holding you here."

"I know," the elf says not looking up from his book. "I feel like I can do more from here."

Barin rolls his eyes, taking off his coat and hanging it up on the coat rack. "You came so you could help me and so that you could get out of that cell. And now you haven't even gone outside. You're going with me tonight."

Alois closes his book; slowly his eyes lift to meet Barin. "Do you want to know the truth Barin?"

Barin comes and sits down next to him on the bed. "Yes I would, I really would. You are my friend, you can tell me whatever it is that is wrong."

"I am afraid," Alois says meekly. "I am afraid to go see what it is like." He turns the book over and over in his hands. "I am scared of how much the city will have changed from when I used to live here. No one I know is here. The inn is gone, my monastery was destroyed. What is left for me?"

Barin doesn't quite know what to say to that exactly. He had been lost when he had first started to explore the city. Not every street that Alois had put on the map was still there, while other roads that hadn't existed had been created where buildings had fallen. It had taken some getting used to, but Barin was able to create an updated map to explore the city with. "I know, this isn't the city I knew either. But maybe it's a good thing? Maybe now that the people have been stirred up more the Fritual will come out?"

Alois shrugs and opens his wardrobe and puts the book away. Then he pulls out another and opens it and carries it over to the desk. He lays the book on the table, opens it to the newest blank page and pulls out a jar of ink and his quill.

"Wait," Barin says covering the blank page with a hand. "Before you make a new entry for today in your journal you need to come see at least part of the city. We won't go far I promise. Then you will be able to take note of something you actually saw versus just things you heard me talk about."

Alois sighs. "Boy there is something about you that I love. That is also the same thing that sometimes I despise about you." Barin grins mischievously and scoops up Alois' journal. "You never stop going and pushing. You like to push people's buttons, don't you?"

Barin pops up and puts the journal back on a shelf in the wardrobe. "Maybe I do, but maybe I like seeing people go out and do things that I know they'll enjoy. Come on, grab your cloak, grab your boots, I know somewhere I have to take you," Barin says turning and grabbing Alois' and his cloaks off the hook. Alois looks at the cloak like it is something that he is going to regret doing. "Come on. I swear it is something that you will enjoy, it's a place you told me you used to visit a lot."

"Where?" Alois asks, pulling the cloak over his shoulders. "I thought just about everything was gone."

"I said just about, not all," Barin replies, pulling their door open. He hurries down the stairs and out into the yard where he waits for Alois to make his way down the stairs. Barin had found this location after days of searching. The city was a maze of slums and squalor, but it still had some features of the white marbled beauty that had covered the city at one time. Alois pads out of the building, squinting as the bright sunlight lights up his face. Barin smiles as Alois pauses and turns his head to the sky, letting the sun soak his face. His eyelids flutter as they adjust to the light shining through Alois' eyelashes.

"I can't get enough of this," Alois murmurs. He slowly opens his eyes letting them readjust before heading over to join Barin.

"You would be able to get more of it if you came outside." He puts up a hand and silences Alois before the words can slip from his mouth. "And opening your window doesn't count." Barin laughs at the look that falls over Alois' face. It isn't one that someone would expect from an elf as old as Alois.

"You are a stubborn elf aren't you," Alois says walking beside Barin. Barin just smiles and signals for his friend to walk with him down the road to the left of the inn. Alois' eyes are wide, as he takes in the sights of the city. Barin thinks of how his heart had leaped and fell as he walked through the city of his youth. It had changed drastically in the last five years.

There was one place, in particular, Alois had spoken about in his time in the cell in the fortress. Barin had spent the better half of the previous afternoon searching for it. Scanning his map he had crisscrossed the area of new roads and ones that had been destroyed by the invasion of the Dark Ones.

Barin had been careful as he traveled, he was sure that his father had sent some men after him to make sure that Barin was doing the mission as he had been sanctioned. It wasn't hard to tell that they were there the first time. They hadn't planned very well; they showed up in the all-black uniforms that they were given. When the people saw them, the enemies that had destroyed their home they fled. Some ran screaming, others scooped up children and ran, or slowly backed away eying them up and down like they were going to pounce on them any second. Barin's tails quickly learned to change up their look. They bought simpler clothes and laid low for a bit. But by that time they had realized their mistake most people had spread the news of what they looked like to the rest of the people.

Barin scans the busy road; he had only had a real run in with them once. It was on his second morning in Bulandon when he ran into them in the black garb. They had all frozen, staring at each other. They all stood and grabbed their blades. When they continued on it was very tense, with many a glance over his shoulder to make sure that the two weren't following Barin. He had kept on with his day, but he had been wary, whenever he had stopped somewhere he had turned in a circle, scanning for people. Others had noticed his paranoia of course, but when he simply said that he thought he had seen members of the Dark Ones in the vicinity, other people switched to the offense. Since then he occasionally would drop this line when he could feel them sneaking up on him, watching his every move.

"So when are you going to tell me where we are going?" Alois asks.

Barin glances over at his friend. "You will know exactly where we are going when we get a bit closer."

Alois eyes him, glancing around at the area. Barin can tell that not much of it is familiar, but Barin can see the occasional flash of recognition from Alois. They might have been the of smallest details, but his eyes widened ever so slightly with each gargoyle high on the wall, or design set into the uneven cobblestone street.

"We are going to turn right here," Barin says pointing to the right down a small alleyway.

Alois stops walking. "You found it?" he asks, his body leaned toward the alleyway ready to move as soon as he lets himself, but he is tense from head to toe, afraid to move to the place of his past.

"I did," Barin replies. "It was sort of hard to find, but once I found it, it seemed obvious where it would be." He starts to take a step forward then realizes just how tense his friend is. "Do you want to go? We can go look at some other stuff first."

"No, no," Alois says, his eyes in the past. "No I want to go. I need a moment." He looks around the entrance to the alley trailing a hand down the wall, remembering the uneven texture of the stones beneath his finger. "It seems like it was so much longer than five years."

"I know," Barin says, placing a hand on his shoulder. "Take however much time you need."

Alois shakes his head. "No, we don't have to wait. I am ready," he says turning to Barin, "let's go."

Barin nods and the two turn. Barin lets Alois lead, so that he can go at the pace that he needs to go. The ground beneath their feet is torn and uneven where the ivy and hedges have been ripped up. Alois slides his hands over the walls tracing the now faded words that are etched in a soft cursive. "Spiriatio fritual per da Bulandon," Alois whispers as his finger runs over the words. Alois continues past the words then pauses just before the opening to the courtyard beyond. "Barin do you know if anyone else has been found?"

Barin shakes his head. "It is something I am working on trying to find out; I don't know what happened to them, whether they ran away to safety or if... I will find out for you."

Alois nods and looks forward. He takes a deep breath then steps forward. When Barin's eyes adjust, he sees the clearing as Alois must have seen it nearly every day when he had been a monk to the Spirit Fritual. He would have come into this courtyard to read and write, on nice days he could have eaten and watched the birds flit around in the fountain. Alois had told Barin that at one point the fountain had sent water ten feet into the air, misting the water out to the rest of the courtyard. Now the water is stagnant, turned to deep green as moss grows across the fountain's base and up the second bowl. Alois steps over the cracked, uneven cobblestones and sits on the edge of the fountain. His eyes drift around, and Barin can't help but think he sees both worlds at once. Part of him wants to speak to Alois, but he feels that he shouldn't pull Alois from this moment. It was a time he would want to remember so he could write down every detail. Barin didn't want his friend to forget his world, as it was and what it had changed into.

"Brother Bruno used to sit over there," Alois says pointing over at a stone bench that has fallen, the broken halves stabbing the sky. "He would write for hours, and sing as he did, I never understood how he could focus on both things at once. He always liked to sing the hymns about hate. That was another thing I couldn't understand. It did sound good when he said them in his deep baritone, but they were so sad and somber. It was never the type of song I would have thought to sing when you would be sitting out here." He pats the edge of the fountain. "I wanted to bring the Fritual here, to sit him or her down here and show them all of the books that I loved, the books that had taught me so much about what they were and what they could be."

Barin comes and sits down beside him on the bench. "You never know, you could still get that chance." He glances around. "I mean that is the whole point of us being here right? What would you want to tell them if it was them sitting here beside you instead of me?"

Alois closes his eyes and leans back like he is cataloging everything he knows and decides what he would want to tell them first. "I would tell them how special they are. That they are so different from all the others, their powers are in the realm of, well obviously, the spiritual versus the physical. They can—" He pauses suddenly and when Barin's eyebrows knit in confusion at the sudden pause, Alois nods in the direction of the wall through which they had come.

The two Dark Ones that had been tailing Barin for days are standing there in the archway. "Lord Barin," the one on the left says, casually resting his hands, one on his hip the other on the pummel of his sword. He makes it look like it is nothing but Barin knew from the many different training sessions he had gone through that the elf could pull out that sword at the blink of an eye. "I don't believe that this was the mission that Lord Nurzan sent you on."

Barin bites his lip trying hard not to respond with the fact that

176

neither he nor his father were actually lords. "I didn't know my father sent me a pair of nannies to watch over me while I was away," he retorts, rising from his seat on the fountain. He wasn't going to let them think that they were scolding him like a child.

"Your father wants to be allowed to trust you, but his generals advised him that it would be a good idea to make sure that you were doing your job," the second guard says. He is not as well trained as his partner, he grips the blade, his knuckles white from the force of holding his sword.

"I have slowly been searching and scanning the city. If you hadn't remembered none of us have been in the city for five years," Barin snaps. He has no patience for these bullies. "Many things have changed. I don't appreciate you following me around everywhere I go. It makes it rather difficult for me to get people to trust me when a pair of men who are supposed Dark Ones are following me." The two guards shrug, not caring at all. "I have been learning the land and starting my search, Alois has been sitting in the room for days while I go around. So as I had come across this location as I traveled. I knew that this place would give me some information to look out for." As he speaks the two guards slowly shrink. Alois turns and is watching him as he speaks. "Do you even realize where we are? How dare you think this is not me working for the good of the mission? So why should you think following us was a good idea? If someone sees us here, they will not talk to me, and then that will be on you. I don't think my father would appreciate that fact too much." Barin's chest rises and falls in anger that he doesn't realize he feels. Pushing it aside he turns to Alois, he is giving him a queer look of pride, but almost fear.

"Maybe we did make a mistake," the elf to the left says.

"There isn't a way you can correctly work if we are hovering."

Barin tries to keep a straight face, but he has to glance over at Alois. As he watches the two Dark Ones, their faces are falling into a soft, droopy look, almost like they are falling into a deep trance in front of them. "We should go," the second one says grabbing the arm of the first. "Come on, let's leave Lord Barin to himself." They walk with arms that swing limply at their sides. It is like someone has reached in and wiped away any trace of a mission from their minds and instead filled them with doubt and cowardice.

Barin and Alois watch in amazement as the two guards turn and walk down the alleyway and out the door with not so much as a single glance back over at the pair by the fountain. Barin turns to Alois, a mixture of fear, understanding, and confusion played on his face. "Alois what the hell just happened?"

32

Ward

"Ward. How have you been?" A guard slaps Ward on the back in greeting. "What shift they got you assigned to?"

Ward swallows the chunk of bread he has been working on and says, "Hello Gleason, I'm tired. Wish we were being paid to do this. I did fewer hours on the farm and was just as tired. They have me assigned to watch Miss Taytra Flynn."

Gleason releases a hearty laugh. "Damn, I hear that she is a handful." He stops to think. "Remember those classes last year when she would interrupt the teacher at least twice a class?"

Ward smiles. "Sure, she has an attitude. She knows she does, she knows how to work it to her advantage."

Gleason leans forward "So how crazy is she? I heard she screamed and fought for hours when she was separated from her father."

"You seem to base a lot of things off of rumors," Ward says dryly.

"Well there isn't much else I can base things off of is there? So? How did she react?"

Ward exhales, picturing the fear in Taytra's eyes when the

black coils of magick wrapped around her. "She's scared. Her sister is gone, not only that, but she has been run out of her home by people who want to kill her. Now she is being held as bait for said sister. And now she has been separated from her father. You have a little sister Gleason." Gleason nods. "Think of how she feels." Ward pauses to take a calming breath and realizes several other guards are listening. "You may enjoy your time here, for the food or the structure of it, whatever. But I want my old life back. What parts I can have back at least."

"What are you saying, Ward?" Andrew, Ward's childhood friend, asks sliding onto the bench beside Ward.

"I am saying what I feel. I hate that my siblings are locked up somewhere below."

"Surely you have seen them. We all have gone down to see them," Gleason sneers.

"Of course I have, but I hate the idea that they are locked up in a cell while we get to roam around this giant castle with so many hallways you could get lost." Ward decides that at this moment he can't plant the seed. Gleason has taken to the Dark One's movement too heavily. Slowly at meals for the last few days, Ward had been dropping hints. Andrew knew the truth, Ward had spoken with him in the barracks. This was the type of man for the false trail, the one they wanted the guards to pick up on. "To be honest, I just want to leave. I want to take my family, and Taytra and leave."

"What?" Gleason says. "That's treasonous. You will get yourselves killed."

"Is it truly treason if they don't rule over me?" Ward counters.

Gleason jumps up slapping his specially issued guard's cap on, it was identical to every man here, but Gleason wore it like it was a privilege to don such a wonderful metal helmet. "Yes,

Ward it is. I would watch yourself if I were you." He spits before hurrying away.

"Why I know he's gonna do it for me," Ward whispers to Andrew.

"You be careful with that one." Andrew murmurs back.

"I will don't worry." Ward grabs a few bread buns from the table and shoves them in his pocket. "I am going to switch with Sam," Ward says rising from the bench.

"You know if I," Andrew starts.

Ward puts a hand up. "Whoa, don't, don't say it." He smiled. "No, I'll see you later Andrew." He leaves the table and feels the eyes of the guards follow him. *Good, let them follow me and think.* Join him against the Dark Ones in our rebellion. He wonders how long it will take for word to go to the higher ups. He goes through the halls that once were filled with light, but in little over a week it has turned dark and dirty. The first day he had walked through these halls he had been astounded by the high vaulted ceilings and the light and grace of the place. Now darkness is in control. The spaces feel smaller; thoughts aren't safe and free.

The dungeons were always dark, but now they feel dank and dreary, Ward doesn't know how it had felt before, but the dark magick on the locks sucks all the light from the torches.

Sam stands beneath a torch pressed against the wall to stay within the flickering ring of light. The young boy should never have been taken from his mother. "Who goes there?" Sam calls down the hall, whipping around at the sound of Ward's echoing footfalls. "I said who goes there?" Sam says adjusting the helmet that continually falls to cover his eyes.

"It's Ward," he calls down the hall.

Sam's body relaxes slumping back. "Oh good, I didn't want to try to use this," he says gesturing at the spear leaning against the wall beside him whose point hovers a good foot above his head.

"No need to be so jumpy, Sam," Ward says patting him on the shoulder. "How's our charge been today?" he asks looking over at Taytra's sleeping form.

"She slept, then ate her breakfast, then we talked for a bit. She wanted to know if any of us had seen her father. But he is in the tower right?" Ward nods. "Right, so we don't get assigned there. I told her that, and she was really sad. She started coloring in the dirt again like yesterday. Then she went back to sleep," the little boy says trying to sound older and official as he makes his report.

"Perfect, Sam."

"Ward? Is she going to be okay? It is so lonely down here; it has to be so scary down here at night. It can be scary during the day, so the night it must be ten times worse."

"Sam, that is why you are here."

Sam scrunches up his little face contemplating what that could mean. "Huh, I thought my job was to make sure she doesn't get out."

Ward smiles and nudges Sam's helmet. "Well, that is what they will tell you is your job. But wanna know what I say your job is?" Sam nods his helmet furiously bobbing just a second slower than the rest of him. "I say that your job is to protect her. You must protect your friend from the dark and the things that lurk there. You are there to comfort her in this very hard time. We need to be there for each other. How does that sound?"

Sam grabs his spear and stands nice and tall. He opens his mouth to speak, pauses, fixes his helmet then goes on. "That sounds great. I can do that, Tay is my friend. I like your version better."

"I can take over from here now, go on they are still serving dinner."

"Thanks, Ward." The boy grabs his things and takes off down the corridor. "See you tomorrow," he calls over his shoulder.

Taytra rolls over, a gleam in her eye. "You are great with him."

Ward slides down the wall resting his hands on his knees. "How long were you awake?" he asks pulling out his knife and a small block of wood. He is slowly, over the course of these watches, shaping it into a small dog.

She sits up and shakes out her long blond hair, picking out the bits of hay that have laced their way into her hair. "Since he called down the hall. I chose not to move until I knew who it was." She quickly twists the strands into a thick braid and ties it off with a bit of blue fabric from the bottom of her dress. "Then when I know it was you I decided just to wait and listen."

"And?" He asks, peeling a large sliver of wood off his carving.

"Well, I can tell he really looks up to you. You are like a big brother to him." She pauses, her thoughts spinning to the thoughts that creep into her mind when she is alone. Carefully she stretches her fingers between the bars and picks up a sliver that has fallen from Ward's work. "Do you think all of this will work?" The shaving is thin and pliable. She begins folding it in half then in half again, and again, and again.

"Tay," Ward replies softly sliding closer to the bars, which hums sensing his proximity. "I will get you out of here. I promise you that I will." He wants to hug his friend, dirty and sweaty as she is. "I won't let them keep you here."

Taytra reaches between the bars again, touching his finger-tips. "What's happening up there?" she asks staring hard at his hand.

"We are getting there. I planted our false trail today. Gleason, he is so caught up in it all that I am sure it won't be long now."

"You are sure that they will come with us?" she whispers.

"No one likes the fact that their family is locked up or being threatened constantly. I don't know if they will come for you and your family, but maybe they will come for their own. Andrew is regularly put down with the families being held here, so he is our go- to for that."

Taytra shifts to rub her arms. "So now we just need to wait and see?"

He nods. "We just need to—"

"WARD!" A voice cuts through the silence, Taytra jumps and grabbed the bars while Ward launches himself to his feet.

"What was that?"

"Ward, Ward help!"

Taytra and Ward crane their heads listening hard. "Was that Sam?" Ward asks before jumping away from the bars as the viscous black magick floats towards him. "Taytra let go of the bars!"

She tugs her hands, the muscles under her skin visibly straining "I—I can't! Ward help, I can't let go." Her eyes grow as fear overtakes her. "Ward go, run!"

"Ward help!" Sam's voice is closer accompanied by heavy footsteps.

"Shut up boy," the elf barks. "Your warnings won't help your friend now."

Ward shudders as the coils wrap around him cooling his skin wherever they touch. "Ward go, run deeper into the dungeon."

Ward takes a deep breath trying to relax his pounding heart. "No if I don't fight them they will go away," He says trying to sound more confident than he feels.

"Nice try boy," the man says throwing Sam to the floor. "I control this magick now." He twists his hand, and the coils wrap a little tighter around Ward's shoulders, slithering to his neck. "Now I have heard some rumors about you boy. I chose to ignore them, pinning them simply on the fact that you are new and these aren't ideal circumstances. That was until this one …" He kicks Sam who scurries back into the ring of light. "Was heard upstairs bragging about what you said were your real duties. So I thought we would have a look. And what did we find?" He glares at Taytra, and new coils pool in his hand and begin wrapping themselves around Taytra's arms. "We find you, getting a little comfortable with your charge. What do you have to say for yourself?"

Ward takes a deep breath hoping the coils might respond. "She is my friend." Ward says.

"Your friend. You are putting you and your family at risk for your friend," the dark elf scoffs.

Ward's breathing is becoming more difficult; dark spots are starting to dance in his vision. "If I didn't I would be wronging all that my family has taught me."

"Ward, stop this," Taytra says through gritted teeth still trying to free her hands.

The elf flicks his hands over, and the door opens and lifts Taytra into the air. "Sam, go and rally the guards. Now we get to go have some fun."

33

Shauna

I pop my eyes open once I am sure that the elf sent to watch me has finally left the room. I jump up from the bed I have been confined to for the last few days and feel my head spin. Amicus had to bleed me to get the poison out of my system. I am grateful that I am better, thankful to be alive but I really don't like how weak I feel. The weakness is what has confined me to the bed for the last two days. I grab the door frame to steady myself as the ground ripples beneath my feet. "Shauna, what are you doing up?" Paulo asks catching me from the corner of his eye.

I can't help but groan. Every time that I have gotten up from the bed, Paulo has caught me and sent me back to my little room. He is like a goody two shoes big brother who won't give me a break. "Paulo, come on. I am going stir crazy in there. Please let me sit out here with all of you. We have things we need to plan and get ready to do." I advance into the room and plop onto a chair at the table where he sits. I may have moved a little too quickly, but I do my best not to show it. "Besides, I'm really hungry. Not chicken broth. Food." My stomach growls, to reiterate the point.

"You are such a pain. Do you understand how scary all of this was? You could have died. You almost did!"

I put up a hand still wrapped in the bandages. "Paulo, believe me I know, I don't think I could ever forget. I have multiple scars from it. But think about it, this was week one. We have so much more to do, tomorrow could be your day to almost die. This isn't going to be easy. We all know the risks." I grab a pear from a bowl of fruit on the table, and take a big bite. "Now, I am starving, those herbs that Amicus used just burned through my system."

Paulo sighs. "I'll tell Amicus you are up and see what we can do. You missed lunch by just under an hour. I'll see if they have some leftovers." Paulo leaves glancing over his shoulder as he does so, making sure that I stay rooted in the chair.

"So he finally let you out of your room?" Lyra asks.

I smile. "I sort of put my foot down." I take another bite of pear and look at the girl in front of me. She is much older than me, I know that without a doubt. I can't remember just how much older - my memory still has holes. I could have sworn that Paulo is the younger of the two. She is just a bit older and wiser. More knowledgeable in the ways of the world. "I suppose, I should thank you," I say softly.

"Why would you need to thank me?" Lyra asks. "I should be the one thanking you. You have done so much for me already."

"What? How have I done anything for you? All I have done has been poisoned and almost died, you, on the other hand, have done so much for me. You helped Paulo to rescue me, then knew where to go. Amicus may have been the one to administer the drug that saved me, but it wouldn't have mattered if you hadn't helped me to get here. You saved me, I owe you my life twice over really."

Lyra nods accepting the claim. "My friend, you have more to your credit than you know. I have been alone for a very long time. My people were there first to fall to the Dark Ones. I didn't know if I would ever find the other Frituals. Imagine finding three of you at once. I feel overwhelmed and overjoyed. Now that we are waiting and letting you heal, I can really let the feeling take hold. I don't have to be alone, for I have found my new people. You, Shauna are to thank for that."

I take a few more bites trying to piece together a coherent reply, but I don't want to deny her. There is genuine gratitude in her voice. "Lyra, how have the Dark Ones not found us yet? They were right behind us weren't they?"

Lyra shakes her head. "I don't really know. Maybe there is a sort of protective spell over the place? Amicus won't really say, he just said not to worry and that we are protected as long as we stay indoors. I don't like it much. I can't feel the changes in the air."

I smile around the bit of pear I have taken a bite of. "Amicus didn't really say, or he won't really say?" I turn the pear core over in my hands looking for one last sweet bite.

"The first one, he doesn't want to give away all of the secrets about this place. It is too special to him."

I carefully balance my pear core on its end so none of the sticky juices get on the table. "Was this really his home? Matron's home?"

Lyra nods. "The people who are brought here are healed where it is best needed, but once they start to recover they are taken to the room you slept in. It was his room,"

"I have been sleeping in his room?" My thoughts fly to the story I had heard over and over as a child. "Was this the cottage where they lived together?"

"No, no that cottage is still missing to my knowledge, perhaps it is a branch of this house of healing, and it abides by the same rules of secrecy."

I am speechless for a moment. "Lyra, this is all so amazing. I've heard the story so many times. I always wanted to find his home, to feel like I was a part of the story in some way. I never thought it would be like this. Maybe that is why I always had a fascination with it. Maybe it was my subconscious that knew, and that was its way of telling me." We sit in silence for a few minutes listening to the soft movements of others in the cabin. "Do you have any idea how long I have to keep resting?"

"As long as it takes," Paulo says carrying a tray of food in front of him.

"Paulo," I groan. "Come on."

"Shauna you're okay!" Philippe pops around the corner and squeezes me, a little too tight. "You are okay right?"

I laugh at how ridiculous he is being, pushing him off. "I am okay, when I can breathe at least."

"Right, sorry." He takes a step back trying not to look too worried. "Amicus told me that I should sleep, that he would tell me if anything was wrong, but he wouldn't give me any updates about anything."

Paulo laughs. "Because you were nagging him to no end."

Philippe shrugs trying to play it off like it is nothing. "Well, you know I was worried. She was stabbed, and he made it sound pretty bad."

I look down at the bandages that ring my wrist. "I wasn't so much stabbed as poisoned." I hold up my other wrist of bandages. "Amicus is the one that cut me."

"Right," Philippe says looking uncomfortable "I was hoping we wouldn't have to cut you if the water worked."

"But it did work, Amicus said that was probably what ensured that I would live." I turn to Paulo, "Alright, what do we have for some lunch?"

Paulo puts the tray down carefully then flicks the cloth off the top of the tray revealing the goodies below. "Carrots, mashed potatoes, and a roast. Which if you don't eat I will. It was fantastic."

My mouth begins to water instantly when all the smells hit me. I search the table for a fork and knife. "There won't be a crumb left, don't you worry," I say digging in. The meat is like butter, so tender that it falls apart beneath my fork. "This is unbelievable, my compliments to the chef," I say. Philippe glances at the other two, and they nod and back out of the room. I let my gaze follow them out. "Where are they going? I thought we were going to work on planning what to do next? I can't stay here forever you know."

He pulls out a chair and sits next to me. "We are planning, we aren't going to stay here forever." He takes a deep breath. "Shauna, the others and I talked. I told them but we— I feel that we can't go forward until you all know my story. Paulo and Lyra heard me out, but you are the one that was really betrayed before. And I need to fix that."

I take a deep breath. I knew this is coming, he is right of course. This is a conversation we need to have, but I was hoping I could put it off for a bit longer. Maybe forever. "You are right, we do."

He relaxes a bit, like just getting me to talk to him about was something that he had feared to begin. I wait for him to start. I have missed his eyes.

"Alright... so I guess it goes back to the test. When I jumped in the water. I thought I heard voices when I was in the water, it was confusing they were saying that I didn't belong here and that I needed to leave."

"You didn't say anything about that?" I cut in. "You didn't even look nervous, and you proposed."

He shrugs. "You didn't say anything about being the chosen one either. Besides, if you hadn't been the chosen one and I came up and told you I heard voices you would think that I was crazy." I shrug, then nod. I would be pretty concerned if anyone told me that they heard voices. "Exactly."

"So we went to the city and went our separate ways. I got changed and bathed, but when I went to find you, they said you had left. I thought that was odd, 'cause we were going to explore together, so I went back to my room. I was pretty mad at you," he confesses. "How often did we get to go to the city, together I mean. There were so many people and no one would have noticed us. Then there was the ceremony." He takes a deep breath. "You really hurt me, Shauna. I think I was still mad about what had happened earlier but, saying you wanted to try this even if it might cost us, us. That hurt more than anything."

My face burns. This is the part I don't want to talk about. "I was trying to keep you safe. I didn't know what was going to happen to me. I just wanted what was best for everyone," I whisper.

"But you didn't even give us a chance."

"It was what I was told to do. I didn't want it but now it almost makes sense."

"By who?" he snaps. "What did the queen know about you that I didn't?"

"She didn't want people to use people that I loved against me. Look how well that worked out," I say bitterly.

He runs a hand through his hair. "I am sorry, I didn't mean to yell at you. I want to talk not fight."

"It's okay," I whisper. "It hurt me too."

"I believe you," he says. He started to put his hand out, maybe to take mine, maybe to push hair away from my face like he used too. Whatever he had been thinking he lets his hand drop back to his lap. "All the anger and pain I felt went into my hand when I grabbed your shoulder. All the heat in my face left suddenly, and you were burned." He breaks off wringing his hand. "Amicus told me that my powers are more connected to my emotions. So I need to stay calm, it doesn't matter if I am angry or scared or upset, it could be the spark." He touches the wrist that is wrapped in cloth and a poultice for a burn. "That's what happened with this one. I was scared, scared I was going to lose you again."

I turn my hand over and take his hand. "I am here now."

His eyes jump to her face. "Do I have you?" he asks softly, waiting carefully for my answer.

I duck my head and look at our hands, my hand feels so comfortable in his. It is something familiar. "I don't know. Tell me what happened after the ceremony."

His shoulders slump. "I am so sorry about what happened. If I could take it all back, I would I-"

"Philippe," I interrupt, "I need to know what happened." I take a deep breath. "I am going to say something, and you won't like it, but I need to say it." He nods. "I am scared of you Philippe. That man that did those things is not the man that I know. I was betrayed. I loved you, and you were supposed to protect me. You broke that trust. Now I need you to tell me what happened so that I can maybe start to trust you again."

Philippe starts to say something but the noise catches in his throat. His eyes search mine digging to find... I can't tell what exactly it is he was searching for. He looks out the window, his jaw working, the muscles twitching. My hands feel hot and clammy in his. When I pull my hands away, pain flashes across his face, but after a moment he nods in understanding. Just to be safe.

"After they took you away," he begins, "I was also taken. They took me to a stable and said I had to be taken to Fuegaste Peak to take their test, to see if it was just a mistake or if I really was the Fuegaste Fritual. So they put me on a horse." He pauses and gives a sheepish smile. "You can probably imagine how that went."

I can, Philippe is not a good rider by any terms of the word. We had tried riding together several times, but he was just too clumsy for it. "Oh no, did you fall?" I ask, a tinge of laughter shaping my words.

"No, I didn't fall," he says. "I almost did, but I managed to stay on. But I was slow, I feel like this is the reason everything happened. If I had been faster maybe Damian's men wouldn't have caught up with us. They must have pushed their horses very hard to catch up with us. I thought that they were going to take me back to the castle and put me up there, but they took me to the camp, I don't understand how he was there." He shudders trying to push away the image of the dead man with black veins spider webbing across his body. "I don't really know how he did it, but he got inside my head. I really wanted to believe him, that having these powers was wrong. That we shouldn't have been related to the elves. But we are somewhere down the line. I don't know why I felt that way. I never cared about it before. I never really thought about it. I know we are clearly different people but..." His words fade as he tries to think of a way to put his opinions into words.

"I understand what you mean," I say. "I have been thinking about this as well. I have always held elves above myself. Maybe because their culture is so different or all the stories." I sigh. "I never thought something like this would happen."

"Who could?" he asks. "So you see I never meant to hurt you. Ever. I would never try to hurt you like that."

"Do you still feel it?" I ask softly, dreading the answer.

"What? His power over me? No, no love," he pauses as the word of endearment slips out. "No, the nearer to the end, the more you fought back, the more time passed, the weaker he got, and the more power over me diminished. I remember every moment Shauna. I regret every moment of it. I wish I could take it all back." He looks me dead in the eyes as he says it, trying to show me how truly sorry and serious he is.

"Everyone has the choice to choose good. You knew you were on the wrong side," I say quietly.

34

Taytra

Taytra doesn't like where this is going. The ring of people surrounding her in the middle of this room is growing by the minute. The throne room is still decked out for the Fritual ceremony. The memory stabs Taytra. She had tried to protect her family that night and look what good it had brought her. It was her turn now to stand up on the platform with hundreds of eyes upon her. Ward stands off to the side. It is only slightly annoying to her that he isn't tied up, why do they think it was safer for them if he is loose? *Someone probably told them what happened the last time that you stood on this stage* she reminds herself. She has to give them a little credit for thinking about that one. She really hopes that that man rotted in Hell. *Who did he think he was? Attacking my sister like that. Bastard.* She remembers the big hole in his chest and how the blood stained the blade of the knife after that. *I would do it again if I had too.* She looks around and knows that that time might be sooner than she had once thought. She takes a deep breath and straightens her back, whatever is coming she will be ready for it. She looks over and catches Ward's eye. He scans her face looking for signs that she is okay. When she nods he relaxes and gives her a sort of half smile. He is as clueless as to what is going to happen as she is. She was the first of all the people captured in Cabineral to rebel. She wonders what they had done in the other kingdoms. If there had been no communication between the kingdoms that led to the idea that they are dead, Taytra couldn't help but wonder if she would be the first of many to go. Had others thought to rebel and failed? Did the Dark Ones have a "signature move" or did they change it up as they went?

She freezes as her father and Moraine are dragged into the room. Fear and relief ripple through her in alternating waves tying her stomach in knots. She is overjoyed to see her father, but fear of what they might do to him begins to outweigh the relief. Her father and Moraine look to be alright, tired, dirty. The cut on her father's cheek seems to be healing nicely. She looks over toward Ward, who quickly puts the pieces together. "Breathe," he mouths. She must be an open book to him. She takes another deep breath counting the beats. She doesn't want to be made to look a fool however this goes forward. She wants the people to remember her as they did her sister. *Strong. Just breathe, the worst thing they could do would be to kill me. Then, well at least you wouldn't be in a cage anymore.*

Taytra takes a few deeper breaths making sure to keep her shoulders back, she repeats the little mantra about being dead in her head when the guard who had brought them here came through the doors. Taytra had seen him only once before. She remembers seeing a group of guards talking quietly but in rapid voices. They kept raising their voices as they got excited but quickly had to bring the levels back down with all the people around. At the time she had just taken it as a sign that they were excited about the ceremony, maybe they had known more than everyone else and that the Fritual had been found. No, Taytra now knows that that was a conference of who could finally engage in an attack that they had waited for, for years, maybe even decades. Again, he speaks furiously with a group of the guards, now a mixture of elves and humans. Taytra can't help but think that this is the opposite of how these elves should act. The idea that they are always parading around is that no human should be able to control their magick. On any level, that humans are base creature compared to their beauty, which on some levels she agrees with. The base and the beauty part. They are a magnificent people, but now a portion of them have taken it too far. It strikes her odd then that men are in the guard because how else could they control the locks? Even teaching Ward how to deflect the coils, so they relaxed had to have been a sort of magick... right?

The guard walks tall and proud to the stage, he wears his all black guard uniform, but he wears a cloak over the top that looks like rippling waves of oil shifting on a piece of fabric. Taytra shoots another glance at Ward. He is rigid, his hands tight in front of him. He catches her eye and ever so slightly shakes his head. This is not good.

She tries to stand tall, Taytra scans the crowd and finds Sam. He is pale, with splotches of heat from anger painting his cheeks. She thinks he has been crying. Sam is quivering, whether from fear or anger, she can't tell from here. She sends a smile in hoping it would give him a bit more courage. Taytra prays he won't be harmed by whatever comes next.

The elf raises his hands like a conductor to an orchestra. The entire room falls quiet, waiting. "Hello, I am Nurzan, general of the Dark Ones." Taytra looks back over at Ward. This is not good, this is definitely not good. "I understand that you here are not quite used to a higher rule. I have been told that you humans had a mayor. I say had because I need to use the past tense. We killed him." There is a cry of pain as Mrs. Pratt, the mayor's wife, learns what happened to her missing husband. "He tried bargaining with us. I don't do bargains." He scans the crowd again. "Then we have the elves, who Moraine more guides through their lives than rules." He gives her a withering glance. "You will find that I am not so lenient. Here we will have rules. Rules that are meant to be followed, not broken. Here ..." He points a long finger at Taytra, then at Ward. "We have two rule breakers. They plotted a way to help her to escape. They are spreading rumors about affection for her. How our rule is wrong. What do you say to this?" Some in the crowd shift uncomfortably. No one wanted to share their true opinion. "Well, this is what I say. I will not kill them" Taytra wants to sigh in relief. However, she can sense that there is more. "But they will be punished. Ward, come here."

Ward steps up tentatively "Yes sir," he says forcing his voice to remain calm.

"I was told that initially, you were a strong soldier. Responsive to all our commands, and orders. You didn't question anything. What changed?"

Ward avoids looking at Taytra staring at a far point on the wall. "I was a good soldier, then I realized that this wasn't the side I wanted to be fighting for anymore."

"What side do you want to fight for?"

"A side where people can be free."

Nurzan glowers down at Ward. "You realize that typically the punishment for being a turn cloak; a traitor— is death." Ward nods. "And yet you still went through with this." Ward nods again. "Well, I must commend you for your bravery and dedication to your cause. I only wish it could have been focused elsewhere. Alas, that is not the case. So we will move forward. Ward is it true that you have grown to care for Taytra Flynn?" Ward glances over at Taytra "Well?'

Ward turns back to Nurzan and says, "I feel that I must protect her. So yes, I care for her."

Nurzan grins. "We can have no more of that. Remove your belt."

Ward freezes looking at Taytra searching for a way to delay the inevitable, but nothing comes to mind. Slowly Ward slips off his belt, loop by loop. "Strip her," Nurzan commands. Taytra tries to fight the hands that grab her, but they quickly strip her of the blue dress Shauna had given her, leaving her in just a short white slip, dirty with sweat and grime from the cell below. Goosebumps of cold and fear rise on her skin as she is forced down in front of Ward. "Fifty Lashings, Ward when you are ready."

"Fifty or Fifteen?" Ward questions, his voice thick, the leather belt hanging loose in his hand.

"Why fifty, of course, this is a punishment is it not?" Ward is frozen, pain painted across his face. "What, does someone need to show you how it is done?" Nurzan asks sarcastically. He grabs Ward's belt and before the man can react brings it down across Taytra's back.

Taytra bites her tongue to stifle her cry of pain. "What too light?" Nurzan asks bringing the belt down again, harder this time. Taytra whimpers and tries to crawl away, but two guards grab her and hold her in place. "That is how you give a lashing," he says handing the belt back to a dumbstruck Ward. "Oh and those two lashings don't add to the overall count." He shoves Ward forward a few steps.

"Tay, I, I don't want to do this to you. I ..." Ward is at a loss for words. "Tay I can't."

"It's okay Ward." She looks away, takes a deep breath and tenses up her whole body. "It's okay, just do it."

Ward slowly lifts the belt and lightly strikes her shoulders.

"Come on boy. You can do much more than that." Taytra tenses up her body again, and Ward strikes again a bit harder. Taytra bites back another whimper as the stripes across her back begin to overlap. Taytra had broken her ankle before. This is worse. She feels where the first part of the belt connects with her skin, and where the rest of its length comes down milliseconds after. It is a pain that lingers spreading across her skin until her entire back burns.

"Please, I think that she gets the point. Please stop," Jamie shouts trying to rush forward. He is quickly subdued by two more guards.

"He will not stop, would you rather we killed your daughter? That is your other option." Jamie settles back reluctantly.

Taytra can see through the tears that she suppressed that Ward is watching her father. Jamie nods. Ward turns and looks at Taytra "Five more," he whispers. "That's it."

She nods, this was it. Ward brings down the belt, again and again, quickly getting the pain away. Then he freezes, arm raised to strike again. "Stop!" Taytra shouts. She grits her teeth and pushes her guards away and forces her way right in front of Ward. "What happened to the boy that was going to protect me?"

He shoves her away, and Taytra stumbles, exaggerating how hard he pushed her. "Do I look like I had any other choice? You try to face him down," he snaps.

Taytra tilts her head toward her two shadows, and Ward nods.

"I trusted you!"

"Will you two please contain the girl?" Nurzan asks lazily.

The two guards in question move forward to grab Taytra. She uses the movement to her advantage. She feels her back stretch and burn as she drops by. She ignores the pain as she falls to the ground swinging her leg around, knocking the two guards from the ground. She jumps up darting for the spears they had been holding, but neither move to stop her. The one on the left winks at her. "Let's go Tay," he whispers, and she pretends to punch him. Before snatching up the spears and tossing one to Ward. "Now!" she shouted.

All around them guards start to fight the Dark Ones. Taytra looks around and sees that all the ones that are on their side pull out a blue cloth and wrap it around their wrists. "Tay let's go!" Ward says grabbing her wrist. She hisses in pain, she reaches around and feels her back starting to grow damp.

"What about Father?" she asks as he pulls her from the room, she turns looking as they run.

"Tay, we need to go. Andrew was going to try to get your father and Moraine." He pulls her into a side hall, and a bunch of elves run by, one glances at them but nods and keeps going. "Tay, I saw some guards pull them from the room before us, but I don't know what side they were on." He pulls his jacket off and drapes it over her shoulders.

"Ward." The two of them jump and press against the wall. "It's me," Andrew calls.

"Here." Ward pops his head around the corner.

"Tay," Andrew says slightly out of breath. "I am sorry. Our people didn't get him. I am sorry. I don't want to rush you but here." He shoves a pair of black pants and a cap at her. "Put those on." He sticks his head out around the corner watching for Dark Ones. Taytra pulls the shirt close, and the pants and hat on her head, tucking her hair into it. "Alright, let's go. We have a few horses ready."

"What about everyone else? The families."

"Some of the ones I thought I could trust know where to go. Right now we need to get the two of you out," he says pulling Ward and Taytra around the corner.

"How many horses, are ready? Who's down there?" Ward asks, a firm hand on Taytra's.

"We have three for us, and then for the families. There are some stable boys down there, but all the guards were called up top for the little spectacle. So that is why we need to hurry so that we can get out of here before the Dark One's catch up with us."

The three of them run into the courtyard where two stable boys hold the horses. "Ward, Ward please take me with you." Ward had given a Taytra a leg up onto a horse when Sam comes running down the stairs.

"Sam, oh my god I am sorry. Please hurry," Ward says grabbing the boy. "Tay, can he ride behind you?"

"Of course, Sam," Taytra says getting herself settled. Ward throws Sam up behind Taytra. "Please just be careful. My back."

"Of course!" the boy squeaks, putting his hands on her waist trying to be careful of where to put his hands.

"Let's go," Ward shouts kicking his horse on and out into the night, the other two hurry behind him and into the city as the rumble of Dark One's shakes the castle behind them.

The rebellion had begun.

The Frituals: Rebellion Coming Summer 2019

The Frituals: Rebellion

Taytra hisses into the pillow, as the bandage comes off her back with a slight ripping sound as the layer of herbs that had been slathered on her back releases.

"This is looking so much better, Taytra," the healer says.

Taytra grunts quietly in reply as the healer grabs a sponge and begins cleaning the bruises and cuts that are left over from the belt marks Ward had been forced to leave on her back. "I think we won't have to put any more bandages on today. You just have to take it easy and let your body get back to moving like normal."

"Thank you, I appreciate all that you have done to help me," Taytra says waiting for the woman to leave.

"Of course, Lady Taytra," she says with a bow.

Taytra sits up clutching a blanket to her chest. "Jean."

"Yes Miss?" Jean asks.

"Remember, just Taytra or Tay. I am not a lady," Taytra says with a smile.

"Right, sorry miss, uh Taytra," Jean says before ducking out of the tent.

Taytra slides off the bed and moves across the floor to a mirror, turning to see her back. Some of the bruises are starting to turn to a disgusting greenish yellow, some are still a dark purple. The swelling has all but disappeared, and as Jean had said the cuts have healed over. She pulls open a trunk of dresses someone had found for her and pulls out a very loose gown that feels like a nightgown. She drops the blanket and pulls on the dress and cinches it just under her chest with a half corset.

The knock on her tents pole is muffled by the fabric but the fabrics bounce alerts her to what she has been waiting all day for. "Who is it?" she calls quickly tying off the corset.

"It's me," Ward says, "can I come in?"

"Yeah come on in," she says tugging at the edges of the corset to make it feel more comfortable.

It still surprises Taytra how much it comforted her to see him out of the black of the Dark Ones uniform. He had even gone as far as to start to grow out a beard.

Ward ducked into the tent, "how are you doing?" He asks, sitting down on the only chair in the tent.

"Well, as you can see I can wear dresses again," she says doing a little twirl. "But I would rather just wear pants. The movement is so nice."

"How bad are the bruises?" he asks quietly.

"Ward, it wasn't your choice. It was what they wanted you to do. We used it to our advantage." She waits until he looks up from his hands before she continues. "They are coming along. Most of the bruises are green and yellow now. I should be fine in the next week or so," Taytra says sitting down on the bed. "I feel a lot better than I did, I feel more mobile. It's nice to not feel like I am going to die anymore." He makes a face at her choice of words. "Stop it," she says punching him. "There is no need for that."

"I am going to keep making faces whenever you talk about how much pain you are in until every bruise and mark is gone."

"What if I said they were all gone tomorrow?" she retaliates.

"I, fine, you win I would still try to make faces."

Taytra sighs and flops back on the bed. She instantly regrets that and has to try not to make a face. Ward leans over to see how she would react. "Oh, stop that," she says swatting him back. "What did you come by for?" she asks.

"I need you to come over to the big tent. We have some new reports that came in," he replies.

"Really? Why didn't you say so? Let's go," she says jumping up and running to the corner to pull her boots on.

"That's a good look," Ward says with a smirk.

"Didn't you know nightgowns and knee-high boots are all the rage in the cities?" she replies grabbing a knife and sliding it into her boot. "Well what are you waiting on?" she asks halfway out the tent flap. She has been waiting for these new reports to come in for days. She starts out into the little tent village they have set up in the woods. Each tent is created in a dark green and brown mottled fabric, so they would try to blend into the woods around them. There is a strict camp fire rule. The only fire allowed to be lit most days is the cook fire. There are too many Dark Ones swarming the area to risk being caught.

Sam's tent is right next door to Taytra's, he is sitting outside on a little stool with a few swords in front of him waiting to be sharpened.

"Good morning Tay," he says. "I just saw Miss Jean leave, your back getting better?"

"Much better, thanks," she says pausing by his pile of swords. "Getting a lot of business, I see." She glances over and sees Ward waiting for her just a few feet away.

"Oh, yea! Each guard or the soldiers that need something sharpened gives me a coin or two to sharpen their swords. I even had an axe this morning. He already came back and got that back. But he said that I did a great job with that. He was going to tell his friends." The pride on the boy's face is contagious.

"That's great Sam! I might need my knife sharpened soon. You know you will have my business as well. I have to go to a meeting, but I'll see you later," she says in farewell.

"Bye Tay." The sound of the whetstone sliding over the blade resumes instantly, slow and rhythmic.

"Any word on his family?" she whispers to Ward when they are a bit farther down the tent line.

He shakes his head. "All we know is that they were seen leaving the palace. It's not certain if they found refuge in the city somewhere or if they made it out around the lake." He glances over his shoulder at the boy. "He showed me yesterday what he's made already. He wants to save as much coin as he can, so he can buy his own sword then go into the city looking for them."

Taytra stops in the middle of the path and grabs Ward's arm. "You can't let him. That boy is not leaving this camp," she says fiercely.

"Tay, don't worry. I'm not going to let him go. Miss Jean is going to keep an eye on him. He is too young to be alone yet, we can't have him getting hurt. Nurzan knows who he is. There is no way they would let him live if he stepped back into that city with the Dark Ones still in control." He pats her hand as he talks and pulls her on. "Come on, we can talk more about what is going on when we get to the big tent."

The big tent is the biggest tent in the camp, serving as the mess hall for the meal shifts, and a planning room for those in charge. Tay doesn't feel like she is in charge of anything but, she, Ward, and Andrew are considered the head of a rebellion. At least that was what was put out in the Dark One's bounties for their return. The rabble that have gathered with them seem to think that this was enough. They named the two men generals and her a lady. It made no sense to her how she went from a farm girl to a lady because she had helped to orchestrate a revolt. Andrew is already in the tent pouring over a selection of paper, and a map of the kingdoms. "Good morning," he says without looking up. He slides his hand along the table looking for a glass nearly tipping it over before getting a grasp on it and lifts it to his lips.

"Hello, Andrew, what has captured your attention?" she asks sitting on the stool beside him.

He doesn't respond at first his eyes staying glued to the page, lips shaping the words. "Huh, oh right sorry, uh it is a report about Nurzan, he left. He went, back to Bulandon. Or at least the Dark One fort near there. The report doesn't say how he got there so fast, but he is gone from our lands." He continues to scan the page. "It seems before he left he ordered everyone on the plain to come here looking for us. So we have the whole of this quadrant on our tail."

"Well wasn't that a lovely parting gift," Ward says picking up another report. "This is our numbers." He scanned the list of digits. "We seem to have slowed down. We have only had one or two people come in the last day and a half." He glances at Tay. "Most are women and children. We can't protect many more. We need more men."

"We have to try to protect them. We have talked about this. Their names are now on their list just as sure as Sam's is. We can't just leave them behind. We might as well be the ones who put the blade in their back," she says vehemently.

Andrew nods. "She is right, they don't have any way to protect themselves."

"And what are we going to do about that?" Ward asks he scans the list again. "We have fifty children under the age of ten in the city, some sixty women and a dozen elders." Andrew and Tay are silent. "We can't ensure they are any safer here with us."

"So we teach them how to protect themselves," Taytra says.

"Tay, there is no way I am putting a knife in the hand of a five-year-old. Do you honestly think their mothers would allow that?"

"Not a knife, as you said we don't have the means to ensure their safety, but we teach them. We teach them how to make little things, traps, and slingshots. There are always rocks around. Nothing is stopping them from throwing rocks at the Dark Ones. They wouldn't have to be anywhere near them," she says trying to make it sound a bit more convincing than it does in her head.

"Okay that's the kids, but the mothers?" Ward says skeptically.

"You might be surprised," Andrew laughs. "You tell a worried mother her child is in danger and she will come up with some pretty interesting ways to attack you. I am sure some of these mothers would be more than willing to learn now to pick up a blade, even if it was just a dagger."

"Besides who said women can't fight?" Tay asks, letting the irony of his suggestion become very clear.

Ward sighs and paces the tent staring deep into the flame of a candle like it will give him the answers he needs. "Tay, have you heard anything from your sister? Not a single word, or random thought?"

"Not a thing, it is really starting to worry me. Are you sure that the Dark Ones said that was a way that they should have been able to communicate?" Tay says staring at the table. "She would have reached out to me by now if she was okay right?" Taytra tries not to let the fear of what could have happened to her sister reach into her voice.

Ward puts a hand on her shoulder. "She might not know she can talk to you that way. There is nothing in the reports that says she has been hurt that I have found. Here." He picks up one and starts reading. "Damian is dead, his body was found on the plateau, the taint of black magic had burned through his veins."

"Wait, how did his body get there? I stabbed him. He died the night of the ceremony." Andrew and Ward share a glance. "What? What don't I know?"

"Tay, uh they reanimated him. He kidnapped your sister and Philippe for a few days."

"What? Was he like some walking corpse rotting away?" she squeaks, she pictures the man she stabbed with green decaying flesh hanging off his body. "Does that make me a killer still?" she asks in a small voice.

"You are not a murderer. You are a liberator Taytra. He tried to kill your sister and a queen. You acted correctly, you had better reflexes than the Elvin High Guard at that moment. That is nothing to be ashamed of," Andrew says.

"Honestly, I thought you were pretty magickal yourself." Ward says with a laugh. "Do we need to have you tested too?" He starts stacking the papers in a pile. "I have gone through most of these, so I will go check on the guards. If you need anything, I will be back in a few."

Tay and Andrew nod. She picks up a random document. Their money. Everyone has been doing what they can, to help. They have an almost self-sustaining community here. Their biggest issues, like one would expect with any revolution, is money for food and weapons. They have just over four hundred maybe closer to five hundred people hiding out in these woods. They all need to be fed and protected in some way. Luckily most of the runaways from the Dark Ones have been able to take their weapons with them as they ran, so they have an odd assortment of spears, quarterstaffs, swords and a few axes at their disposal. But it won't be nearly enough if the Dark One's actually find them. What Taytra is hoping for but hasn't happened yet, is that some of the elves that have come with them would be skilled. That they will be able to control some form of magick or kill in weaponry and be able to teach it to the other elves, or maybe the humans. She knew it was a lot to ask for them to share their learning with Man, but it was a sign that they would truly stand with them.

"Tay, what do you think we will get out of this?" Andrew asks putting down another report.

"What, this revolt?" He nods. "Hopefully a passage back to our old lives. I really just want to make our home safe enough for my sister to come home. If that happened, I would pack this whole camp up by myself."

About the Author

Katelyn Costello started to write when she was 13 years old out of spite. Her best friend got to go to a writing conference, and she didn't. What she didn't know it was that writing conference was more tailored towards poetry and she had decided to write fiction. The idea for her debut novel The Frituals came that following summer. Now 22 and with a creative writing degree from Wells College under her belt (go evens!) Costello continues to write fantasy and science fiction. Living in Rochester, New York with her boyfriend and a new kitten when not writing Katelyn can be found reading, attempting to go on a run, or working in the visual arts as a photographer, stage manager, and lighting designer.

You can connect with me on:
- https://www.katelyncostello.com/
- https://twitter.com/scripturienting
- https://www.facebook.com/thescripturient101/
- https://www.instagram.com/authorkatelyncostello/

Subscribe to my newsletter:
- https://mailchi.mp/946e04db88aa/katelyncostello

16445989R00122

Made in the USA
Lexington, KY
15 November 2018